BEACH MUSIC

BEACH HOUSE ROMANCE
BOOK 5

JULIE CAROBINI

Beach Music (Beach House Romance, Book 5)
Copyright © 2023 Julie Carobini

ALL RIGHTS RESERVED
Dolphin Gate Books

Cover design by Kylie Sek

Library of Congress registration pending

JULIE CAROBINI writes inspirational beach romances from her home on the California coast. Please visit her at JulieCarobini.com.

ONCE UPON A TIME ...

I wrote a series about five siblings who inherited a beach house—with a catch!

That was in 2020 ... and we all know what happened *that* year. Life was turbulent so I decided to do something different: I released all five books under a pen name.

But ... I found it difficult to maintain two personas. I also wanted to add a bit more content to these stories. So I pulled the novels from publication, added new scenes, and re-covered the series under my own name.

If you like tropes, such as fake relationships, billionaires, secret babies, and cowboys, then I know you'll love the revised and refreshed Beach House Romance series!

Now, turn the page for book five ...

Julie

1

Rafael didn't blame the entire town for thinking he was a flake. He gripped the handle of the steel-point shovel he was working with, turned over an expanse of soft loam, piling it high on the ground. Again, he stabbed the earth with the shovel and turned over a pile of dirt. He wiped his brow, then did the same again, the repetition soothing his rising temper. He didn't blame them. Not too much, anyway.

But that didn't mean he had to accept the town's truth as his own.

"Rafael," his brother, Serge, called out. "You gonna be here much longer?"

"Might be." He straightened, aware of his back cracking, leaned on the shovel handle, and tipped his hat backward.

"Why the Stetson? Looks familiar but I can't remember why."

Rafael grimaced. "Sun's hot. Found this among our mother's things." He didn't mention that the hat was his, nor question why his mother had kept it all these years. He'd also found her guitar, and unlike most of the other items that had been hauled off to charity, he'd kept that too.

"Hm," Serge said, pulling him back into conversation. "Maybe the hat belongs to Ace."

"Maybe." Rafael did not care to hear his uncle's name ever again. If the sun weren't so hot, he wouldn't have looked twice at the hat as it, too, reminded him of their uncle. And of his past. But whatever. It served its purpose now, which was to shade him from that beating sun.

"Want some advice, big brother?"

"No."

"I'll give it anyway—maybe give it a rest?"

Rafael stared back at his little brother. There was only a vague resemblance between them. If he watched Serge talking long enough, he would notice the similarly shaped mouth and the fleeting likeness around the eyes. Serge, though, was a couple of inches shorter and stockier than him. This was pointed out to them more than he wanted to think about and he always shrugged it off. Was it anyone's business that they'd been thrown together as a family unlike most?

"In a little while." Rafael gripped the shovel harder now, turned, and dug into the soil again, feeling the tightness in his gut lessening some. His mother was gone and the house he had rented for them would soon be a memory. Despite the difficulties of the past year, he would not leave this place a mess. He would not give the tongues a reason to flap. Instead, he would replant everything that had died while he had been ... preoccupied.

He'd show that landlord of theirs that he came from

good stock, despite the woman's pearl-clutching over the state of her property.

"Isn't being a prostitute enough to redeem yourself around here?"

Rafael looked up sharply at his brother's words.

Serge grinned. "I was just kidding. But you gotta admit, it kinda sounds like that."

"What does?"

"You know." Serge's grin faltered, obviously taken off guard by Rafael's particularly surly attitude. "The auction, man."

Rafael scoffed.

"Or maybe you can't wait for all those women to be throwing their dollar bills at you."

"You think I won't be able to scare up more than pocket change for the shelter?"

"Maybe if you take your shirt off. And hey, I heard they throw underwear sometimes too."

Rafael narrowed his eyes at his brother.

Serge shrugged. "I wouldn't know anything about that, though."

Rafael continued to stare at Serge. Hard. Suddenly, a grin broke through. He scooped up some dirt and pretended to toss it toward his brother. It felt good to grin again, even if it only lasted a moment.

"Hey! I'm just tellin' it like I see it, man. Show those ladies some of that tan skin of yours and the shelter'll be able to pay its rent for the entire year."

"You better watch out, little brother, or I'll drag you up there with me."

Serge pressed a hand to his stomach and laughed until

he convulsed. "Uh, sure." He slapped his belly. "Women love a man who can eat."

Rafael shook his head. "Get out of here." Serge took off, hopped up into his truck, and started up the engine. As Rafael stuck the shovel into the dirt, the sound of it like a shush, he could still hear his brother's laughter. Reality struck him. He was about to go up on the auction block. To stand before the town, available for bidding. If a year ago anyone would have told him this would be his fate, he would have laughed them off. Told them to go and pound sand.

But that was before his mother passed on to heaven. So many believed that he had taken advantage of her, lived off her generosity. He swallowed back the taste of rising bile. His mother was a godly woman, generous with the little she had. And in the end, it amounted to nothing much.

The town didn't know the truth, and quite simply, this auction was Rafael's chance at a redemption of sorts. The animal shelter was in trouble, needed money for back rent and improvements. Any thoughts of changing his mind, of taking himself out of the bidding, fell on the stark reality of that fact. He grimaced. What was a town without a safe place for its lost animals to land?

He almost didn't hear the footsteps. Nor see the girl. Or was she a woman? She slowed to a stop in front of him, an empty leash hanging from her hand, and gave him a curious look.

"Good afternoon. Doing some gardening?"

Rafael took a long look at her. Delicate features. Probing eyes. Confident. Definitely a woman—a can't-take-his-eyes-off-her woman. "I am." He paused. "Are you missing something?"

The woman's perky expression faded some. She took a step away and he feared that he had offended her.

He nodded toward her hand. "I was referring to the empty leash."

She stopped and peered down at the end of the leash, its metal clasp dangling in the wind. The woman looked up. "I'm just out walking my invisible dog."

He sputtered. "Your—"

"Ha! Got you." She laughed in a way that lit up her entire face. Despite the emptiness Rafael had been feeling for weeks, she made him want to smile back.

She continued. "I was out for a walk and decided to buy a leash for my dog. He's at home right now."

"You a new neighbor?"

"Just visiting."

"Ah." Shame. Then again, he wouldn't be around much longer anyway.

"Well," she said, "good luck with your gardening project."

"Thanks." Rafael nodded once at her and watched as she continued past him, heading toward the beach. He called out after her. "Ma'am?"

She swiveled, and even from yards away he could see the question in her expression. "Bring the dog around sometime while you're in town."

Her mouth curled into a smile, and she nodded. "See you."

Rafael watched the young woman stroll away, a slight bounce to her step. Soon the lightness in his heart began to give way to something heavier and dark, a realization that sucker punched him in the gut. He could never have a woman like that in his life—didn't deserve to. He'd made mistakes where women were concerned, many of them, and he dared not think he had earned the right to bring a pure-hearted woman into his life.

He screwed up his mouth, a montage of the last few years running through his mind. *Forget you ever saw her.*

With a shake of his head, Rafael dug the tip of his shovel into the ground again, continuing to dig up soil with the intention of fixing up the yard of a house he didn't even own. The work pulled his mind away from the damsel who had momentarily stunned him with thoughts he had not dared to consider.

As he worked that shovel, his muscles growing taut, he solidified his reasons for taking a stand for those less fortunate in this community—even if the recipients were, well, animals. Allowing himself to be auctioned off to the highest bidder might not redeem his reputation completely, but it sure was a good start.

A DILAPIDATED BEACH house was the perfect place to hide. Bella cuddled Seabiscuit, the Pomeranian-mix pup she'd rescued from the side of a road one lonely night. She tipped up her chin and let the sunlight warm her face. The weathered back porch creaked lightly in the wind, just like old times.

Bella sighed. Kyle wouldn't think to look for her here because she had never mentioned to her ex-boyfriend that this place existed. So ... she had nothing to worry about.

She had come to this old house on a mission. The last of

her five siblings to make the odyssey, so to speak. After their parents died, Bella, her three sisters, and a brother all learned that everything had been left to charity. Everything except this old beach house.

Dad and Mom had also left some quirky instructions in their last will and testament. Each one of the "kids" had to spend a month in the house, fixing it up. Grace, Jake, Maggie, and Lacy had all done their month, in that order.

And now it was her turn.

Her cell phone rang. She scooted Seabiscuit into the house and answered, her middle sister's name on the screen. "Hi, Lacy."

"Hey yourself, brat."

"Nice way to talk to your baby sister."

"The one who made me eat tofu for breakfast last month —and who stuck a bunch of elderberry gummies into my suitcase before I left the beach house?"

Bella laughed lightly and rested her back against her mother's old pink bench. "Just trying to keep you healthy. You have a wedding to plan, you know."

"Yes, well, I want to keep you safe."

"Oh? Do you have reason to believe that I'm not safe in the family beach house?" Bella paused. "I mean, other than the rickety porch and gaps in the walls that let air in occasionally."

"You noticed all that, huh?" The tone of Lacy's voice sounded as dry as soap. "Might want to wear a sweater inside —and keep your phone on you at all times."

"Is this really why you called?"

"No. I was checking in. I had hoped to be back in Colibri

this month while you served your sentence, but as it happens, Finn has other plans for me."

"Honestly, your fiancé is the nicest man. So is Grace's husband, Chase. And Maggie's Luke." Bella sighed. "All my sisters have found the best guys." She didn't add that she was beginning to wonder if there were any more available, though she seriously doubted her prospects. She certainly hadn't come to Colibri with any romantic ideas of her own.

"So you're saying you haven't landed any cowboys up in Washington?"

She hesitated. Bella had never mentioned Kyle to her sisters because, well, in her heart she never saw a future with him. No sense mentioning him now. "Not exactly."

"What about the library? No male bookworms ever approach you for advice?"

"Yes, but they are usually over eighty years old." Bella smiled. She had loved books as a kid, like her sister Grace had. In fact, she would often sneak into Grace's room when they were little and "borrow" books, especially since so many had disappeared in the fire. But she never saw herself becoming a librarian.

Well, a part-time librarian.

"Don't worry, kiddo," Lacy said, "you'll find your prince. But like Maggie always tells you, don't be too gullible."

Maggie was their oldest sister and she always had plenty of sisterly wisdom to share. Her sisters and brother always seemed to shrug it off, but for some reason, her words often stuck to Bella like old wallpaper.

Lacy broke back into her thoughts. "Just promise me you'll have some fun while you're at the house. I think it's in pretty good shape, though I'm sure you'll have your opinions about that."

Lacy knew Bella well. As easygoing as she was, she liked things clean. And chemical-free. "I unpacked all my non-toxic cleaners and essential oils this morning. Cleaning with them does wonders. You'll see."

"Ah. So, the next time I'm there I should expect the place to smell like, what, lemons? Lavender?"

"And oregano, among other things."

"Oh." Lacy laughed. "I was kidding, but I guess ..."

Bella became lost in thought. Lacy was right. She *had* always imagined herself married to a cowboy and living on a ranch somewhere. She'd have a garden to grow vegetables and he'd keep the horses. They would eat beautiful, fresh food together at on old farmhouse-style table—kind of like the one in the family beach house—and live happily ever after. The end.

Why couldn't life be just like the fairy tale she'd always read about in books? Despite evidence to the contrary—her ill-advised pair-up with Kyle, for example—Bella still held out hope that, someday, she'd meet her own Mr. Wonderful, just like her sisters had.

Until then, she refused to stop focusing on *living* in the present, on doing positive things for her community—wherever she determined that to be—and her family.

Speaking of which, she glanced at the flyer that had gotten her attention as she'd walked to the animal shelter earlier today to pick up a leash:

Save the Animal Shelter! Bachelor Auction this Saturday.

. . .

THE WOMAN who managed the shelter, Clementine, had put a sign-up form and pen in front of Bella. "It's for charity. And we're desperate."

What could she do but sign up?

"Hello?" Lacy's voice broke into her thoughts again. "Earth to Bella?"

"I'm sorry. What were you saying?"

"Ignoring me already? I was just telling you where I stashed some haircare products in the downstairs bathroom. I think you'll like the stuff. Maggie picked it up with her industry discount and the shower smelled like a high-end salon whenever I used it."

"Uh-huh. Okay."

Lacy sighed. "And ... I've lost you. Call me if you need anything."

After they hung up, Bella took another look at that flier and wondered where she would get the money to help the shelter.

SATURDAY HAD COME and it was ... show time. Bella strolled into Brooke's Beachside Bakery at fifteen minutes before five o'clock. Her sisters had all raved about the sweet yummies at the new cafe in town. Finally, she had her own chance to check them out. When she told Jake by phone earlier in the week where the auction would be held, even he gave a begrudging nod to the pretty pink bakery in the middle of

Colibri. At the urging of his sweet fiancée, Daisy Mcafee, he also gave her a thousand dollars to spend.

"It's for charity, my love," Bella heard Daisy call out in the background during their phone call.

"Fine," he had said. "Just make sure you get someone who'll help you finish up the work at the house, all right? No freeloaders."

Bella had laughed at that. Freeloaders? That sounded like something their father would have said.

"I'm serious, kiddo."

Why did all her siblings still call her that? Truthfully, she hadn't thought much about the auction itself, how the bidding would go, who she would bid on, etcetera, but one thing was for sure: She did not plan to bid on a guy just to become his date, or worse, his servant. She figured the auction would be filled with the kinds of guys she remembered from her childhood—surfers and super old men with a hammer.

A surfer could be fun. Alas, she had no time for frivolity … no, what she needed was a nice old man with a tool chest. And maybe a broom. Hopefully, by night's end, one would become beholden to her because of her—okay, *Jake's*—generous animal shelter donation.

Cloud cover had cooled the day's temperatures some, so Bella had opted for jeans and boots, a button-down cotton shirt, and a flat brim felt fedora. Basically, party clothes. At least in her mind. Unfortunately, when she glanced around the shop at all the women in sundresses and strappy heels, she experienced a sudden surge of self-consciousness.

"Are you here for the auction?" The young woman at the

entry table wore a big smile and her dark hair in beach waves.

"I am."

"Great! I'm Hattie. What is your name?"

"Bella Holloway."

Hattie gasped. "Oh! You're the last of the Holloway kids, right?"

Bella laughed. "Well, I certainly hope there'll be more of us running around someday. My sister Maggie has already started her family."

Hattie's face reddened. "I didn't mean anything by that. I was just, I mean, you're here to fix up the beach house, right?"

"Yes." Bella shrank back slightly. "Wait ... how do you know about that?"

Hattie grinned and leaned forward. "Everybody knows about the Holloway beach house."

Something twisted in Bella's heart. *Everybody knew?* It did make sense, though. She may have come to town recently, but four other siblings obviously made themselves known these past few months. Hm. Maybe it wouldn't be as easy to hide as she thought ...

"Here's your paddle." Hattie handed her a popsicle stick with card stock taped to it. "Our auctioneer will be calling out dollar amounts. When the bachelor you want to bid on takes the stage, and you hear the number you're willing to pay, just raise your paddle. Highest bidder wins."

"I think I can handle that."

"Some of them are pretty cute," Hattie added. "If I weren't still a poor college student, I'd definitely be bidding. Good luck."

"Thank you."

Bella began moving through the crowd, suddenly aware that she saw not one familiar face among them. Though her sisters and brother had long ago made their homes elsewhere, Maggie had recently moved to town when she married Luke. And Daisy, who would be marrying Jake soon, was often around here since her elderly mother, Wren, lived next door to the Holloway family beach house. She sighed quietly. Maybe she should have invited one of them to join her tonight.

"Eclair?" A woman with decisive eyes and blonde ringlets falling out of her messy bun held a tray of chocolaty goodness in front of her.

Bella bit her lip. She hadn't had dinner yet.

"We need to make sure our bidders are all sugared up for a night of competition." The woman, whose tag read *Brooke*, winked.

Bella relented, helping herself to an eclair. "You're the owner?"

"I am."

"It's a really cute place."

"Thank you! I'm glad you like it. Are you visiting?"

Bella had taken a bite, so she only nodded.

"Nice of me to ask you a question when your mouth was full, right?"

Bella laughed lightly. "I spent summers in Colibri and now I'm—"

"Wait." Brooke's face lit in surprise. "You're Maggie's sister, aren't you? And Lacy's? And Grace's?"

"Guilty."

Brooke put the tray down on a table. "Yay—you're here!

I'm so happy to meet you, Bella!" She pulled Bella into a hug. "I love your sisters—oh, and Maggie does my hair."

Bella held her half-eaten eclair in the air with one hand and hugged Brooke back with the other. So much for being a stranger all alone in this quiet town ...

"That's so nice of you to help the animal shelter while you're here. I just hope it's enough to stave off closure."

"There are a lot of people here already, so I don't see why not."

Brooke pursed her lips. "Well. I hope you are right, but with Lillian, you never know."

"Lillian?"

"Lillian Madsen. The real estate agent who owns the building that houses the shelter." Brooke's eyes darkened and she seemed to assess Bella. "You don't know her?"

Bella shrugged. "Her name does sound familiar, but I'm not sure why."

"Well, I'm sorry to be the one to remind you, but I know she's approached your siblings about selling the beach house."

"The one who tried to sell our house and Wren's next door?" Wren Mcafee and her mother had been great friends. The elderly woman had been recovering from a stroke for months, and from what Bella had heard, Lillian practically pushed her to sell while she was still in the convalescent hospital. Thankfully, Daisy put a stop to that.

She picked up her tray again, a crush of people making their way into the bakery now. "Sadly, yes." Brooke glanced around. "On the bright side, look at all these well-wishers!"

Bella glanced around. "Such a beautiful thing to see."

"I like the way you think, Bella. Have fun tonight."

Brooke sent her a brief wink and then turned to offer goodies to newcomers.

Bella was beginning to wonder if the bakery could hold all the women wanting into this event tonight. The chairs up front near the makeshift stage made of pallets were full and, phew, she'd never seen so much cleavage in one bakery in her life. Maybe she had underestimated the quality of bachelors on sale at this event.

Again, she ran her gaze down her comfy denim and cotton outfit. At least someone was here to bid on one of those sweet old guys from the hardware store.

A squeal of a microphone caused a collective groan. The woman from the shelter, the one with the long ponytail, stood on the stage now.

"Please take your seats everyone!"

Bella glanced around and found an empty seat at a table occupied by several women. She guessed them to be older than her by at least twenty years. "May I join you?"

A woman with teased-blonde hair waved her on to take a seat, her arm bangles clinking together. "Sure, honey." She leaned in close, her perfume tickling Bella's nose. "Have you staked out the one you're bidding on?"

"Me? No. I don't even know any of them."

The woman shrank back. "You're kidding."

Bella shrugged. "I just moved back here and saw the flyer and thought I'd do what I could."

The woman slapped the table, sending up another plume of perfume. Ladies, we have to help"—she looked at Bella again—"I didn't get your name. I'm Kelly."

"Bella."

"We need to help Bella pick her fella," Kelly said to the others. "Ooh, that rhymes!"

A second woman held up her cup of lemonade. "Here, here. I'm Dani. Nice to meet you."

The third woman wore a disgusted pout with her low-cut blouse. "Let me just say, I can't believe we're at a bachelor auction and there's not a drop of alcohol in this place." She turned her gaze to Bella. "Hey there. I'm Casey, by the way."

"Happy to meet you all." Bella slipped her purse onto the back of a chair and it promptly fell onto the floor.

Kelly leaned down to retrieve Bella's purse and gasped. The money Jake had given her had spilled out.

"That's a lot of cash," she whispered, slipping the large wad of bills back into Bella's purse. "You'd better zip that thing up, honey."

"Oh!" Bella felt her face flush. "Thank you so much."

All three women stared at her.

Casey said, "Don't tell me you're planning to buy a guy for every day of the week."

"No, no." Bella began to perspire. "Nothing like that. I-I just wanted to find someone who could help me with some projects around the house. That's all."

Dani gave her an incredulous laugh. "You are so cute and you're going to spend all that on a handyman? For goodness sakes, set your sights higher than that!" She pulled a rumpled paper from her purse, ran her hand down a list, and looked up. "Do you like surfers?"

"Of course. But really, I-I'm not looking for anything other than, you know, some help." A slow sense of dawning arched over Bella as she sat in that room and surveyed the crowd. Except for her, every woman in the room had dressed to, if not kill, at least render their prey incapacitated. Why had it not occurred to her that this simple fundraiser was anything but innocent?

You can be so gullible sometimes.

Maggie's oft-said words flashed in her mind, though she did her best to force them away.

Casey said, "I got it."

Bella, Kelly, and Dani looked her way.

"You need a handyman and I've found the perfect one for you."

Kelly grabbed for the paper. "Let me see that."

Dani pointed at the last one on the list. Casey leaned over and gave an appreciative nod.

Kelly smiled. "Oh, he'd be the perfect one to help you."

"Really? Great! Thank you so much for the guidance."

Someone tapped on the microphone, alerting them that the auction was about to begin. Casey hushed Dani who had turned to a woman at the table behind them. "It's starting," she hissed.

The same volunteer Bella had met at the shelter stood at the mic. "I want to thank you all so much for coming. The Colibri Beach Shelter has long been an institution of hope in this community and"—she paused, composing herself—" and it means so very much that you are here tonight to help us through this difficult time."

Dani put her pinkies in her mouth and blew out a piercing whistle.

Kelly clapped vigorously.

Casey called out, "That's right. You go, girl."

Bella bit her lip. By the looks of things, this was going to be a long night. Hopefully Seabiscuit wouldn't get too rowdy while waiting around in the old beach house for her to come home.

"And now without further ado, let the bidding begin!"

The shop erupted with cheers and shouts to "bring 'em out!" Suddenly, the air in the room blazed with the opening notes of "Cowboy Casanova" by Carrie Underwood and a line of ten men began to strut up the stairs to the stage, across it, and back down the other side.

She squinted, but from this far back, about the only thing she could determine was there was not a single aging, gray-haired man with a hammer in the bunch.

Bella's three new friends stood and began to hoot and holler, clearly trying to outdo the women at other tables. She covered her face with her hands, but at least all eyes weren't on them. She had the bachelors lining up at the front to thank for that.

Dani peeled off a whistle again and added some ground stomping to show her appreciation. Bella peeked out between two fingers and sent up a silent prayer that no one in her group would climb onto the table. She wasn't a prude, but truthfully, she had already stretched her introverted self to come out tonight. Her idea of the perfect evening consisted of a crackling fireplace, a new book to curl up with, and munchies on hand.

What was she doing here again?

Maybe Bella could quietly slip her purse onto her shoulder and tiptoe out. That's it. Tomorrow she would rise early, walk to the shelter, and make a thousand-dollar cash donation. Boom! Yes. It would end up being like a bonus on top of all the money they would surely make tonight.

Slowly, she stood, unhooking her purse from the chair.

Kelly rocketed up and swung an arm around Bella's shoulder. "Where ya goin', honey?"

A couple of whoops went up. Bella and Kelly looked toward the stage. The first bachelor was being displayed like a shiny new car and paddles were popping up all over the room. Kelly cinched her neck. "He's cute, but not the one we're holding for you."

"Thanks, but I think I'm going to go. I left my dog—"

"No-no-no, don't go! You're our party saver tonight!"

"How so?"

"The truth is, none of us really has much money to bid." She laughed. "We're going to try, but you're our ringer tonight."

A gavel collided with the podium. The audience clapped. One bachelor sold.

Kelly cinched her tighter. "Pretty please."

Bella had never been this popular before. Maybe it's because she never had money, but it was more likely because she had never attended a girls' night in a hometown version of Chippendales.

Brooke breezed by holding a tray of lemon bars as another bachelor went up for bid and quickly sold.

Dani and Casey both grabbed one, as did Kelly—only she picked up two and offered one to Bella.

Bella leaned her head to the side and eyed Kelly. "I guess I could stay a little while longer."

"Excellent. Here." Kelly thrust the dessert into her hands. "You'll need this for energy."

For the next forty minutes, Bella watched as bachelor after bachelor strutted across the stage, each garnering bigger praise than the one before. What she wouldn't do to put up her feet at home, sip some chamomile tea, and listen to the waves ...

A murmur went through the crowd. Casey scoffed. Hushed conversation overtook the room, piquing Bella's interest. She squinted at the bachelor who took the stage, the one causing a shift in the room's atmosphere. Something about him looked ... familiar.

But how could that be? She hardly knew anyone around here anymore.

Kelly touched her arm. "Not him. Just wait."

The auctioneer picked up his gavel. "We'll start the bidding for bachelor number seven at one hundred dollars. Do I have a bid for one hundred?"

A paddle went up.

The murmur in the crowd grew, and Bella stood to get a better look. Dark hair, a smattering of stubble across a well-defined chin, eyes that stared, unblinking, into the crowd. No smile whatsoever. Unlike the others, he didn't strut, nor flex a gun, nor do some sort of fake striptease with those narrow, denim-clad hips of his ...

"Oh my gosh, Bella, sit down," Dani said, laughing. "Don't go bidding on the town bad boy."

Casey eyed her warily. "Seriously, hang tight. He's not the one we had in mind for you."

The women reminded Bella of her sisters. She swung a look back toward the stage. The bids kept coming. Two hundred. Three hundred. Even at a five-hundred-dollar bid, bachelor number seven still hadn't cracked a smile. He dipped his eyes, though, a faint light shining on them. Despite the strong outline of his body, the smoldering gaze, he reminded her of a wounded animal. She couldn't pull her attention away from him.

"Five hundred dollars going once."

"Wow," Kelly said, "that's a lot of money for the town Lothario."

Dani fanned herself. "Yeah, he's not a lifer or anything, but I could keep him busy for a few days."

"Five hundred dollars going twice."

Casey shook her head. "He's a boy toy all right, but really not worth all the fuss."

Not worth all the fuss? Bella glanced again at the stage. The man on stage didn't want to be there—she was sure of it. His faraway gaze made him look lost, nearly ready to bolt. She knew the feeling well.

Too well.

As the auctioneer began to lower the gavel, Bella stood, boldness surging within her. She raised her paddle. "One thousand dollars."

Her new friends gasped—collectively. Kelly reached for her paddle, but it was too late.

Bella had just bought herself a bachelor.

2

———

Bella could not quite remember seeing Jake so upset. He was a serious guy, but usually pretty good-natured—at least around his baby sister. Good thing she was looking at him through a computer screen. How did he get his eyes to bulge like that anyway?

Grace chimed in. "I have to agree with Jake here, Bella. Rafael's a good-looking guy—"

"He's hot," Lacy interrupted.

"That he is," Maggie said.

"But all I'm saying," Grace continued, "is maybe he's not the best choice to be your helper. Did you really spend a grand on him? That's a lot—"

Lacy cut in. "How come she gets help, anyway?"

Maggie groaned. "Please. Don't lead us to believe you weren't getting help from your billionaire."

"Only because my back hurt."

Maggie scoffed. "And Grace, too. Chase lived with her

and I'm sure she had him doing all kinds of work around the place."

Grace piped up. "Um, I'm right here."

"All I'm saying," Maggie continued, "is good thing I had Eva to help me, though it wasn't the brawn you all had assisting you."

Grace cracked up. "I'm pretty sure Luke would have helped you if you'd been nicer to him."

Maggie gasped. Her relationship with Luke had its dark moments, for sure, but they were happily married now and all of that was behind them.

Jake grew testier. "Enough! This is a bad idea, Bella. Forget about the money—consider it a donation for a worthy cause and leave it at that. Just stay away from the guy."

Bella checked the time. They were on their weekly family video chat, one of the virtual gatherings they began instituting way back when Grace was the first to fulfill her month at the family beach house. During these meetings, the rest of the family would receive updates of the house's current condition, but instead, her siblings were fixating on her decision-making abilities. The video chat had already run over its usual duration by nearly half an hour.

She ran her gaze over her sisters and lone brother, who all seemed to be arguing about ... her. If this call didn't end soon, Rafael could very well show up here and further upset her big brother.

"So what do you say, Bella?"

She bit her lip. Had they been talking to her? Seabiscuit jumped onto her lap and she began petting the beast. "I'm sorry?"

Jake pointed his gaze at her. "I said, do you agree to tell Rafael his services—"

Lacy laughed at the word *services.*

Jake cleared his throat and continued. "That he's not needed. You'll tell him?"

Bella wrinkled her brow, her mind trying to tackle myriad thoughts. She was about to do her best to calm her brother's fears—unfounded as they may be—when the doorbell rang. Seabiscuit jumped from her lap and scampered away snuffling near the door. He let out a high-pitched whine.

Maggie cut in. "Do you need to get that?"

Bella slid a gaze toward the screen. "Yeah, just a sec." She started walking away, stopped, and stuck her head back in front of the computer screen. "Carry on without me a minute, okay?"

Her siblings' squabbling melded into the background as she made her way to the door, her mind replaying the moments from last night, after her surprise bid brought down the house.

"IT'S YOU," *she had said as Rafael approached her.*

He nodded his head. "Ma'am."

"I met you yesterday, right? In your garden."

His mouth stayed grim, his lips straight. "Yes, ma'am."

She stuck out her hand. "I'm Bella."

Those dark eyes of his lowered, taking in her outstretched hand. A flash of something—fear, maybe?—overtook them briefly. He zeroed in on her. "Holloway?"

His response startled her. He knew her? How could that be?

Then the dawning, like too-bright, sharp rays from an aggressive sunrise, caught her between the eyes.

This was Rafael. The man her sisters had mentioned during the past few months—and the man her brother despised. She remembered him, vaguely, from childhood. She had been too young to pay him much mind when all the older girls were clamoring after him.

And now, he was hers. Sort of.

"I'm not looking for a date," she said.

He nodded.

Bella continued. "I bid on you in hopes that you would spend your week helping me with projects around the house. So I'd like to see you tomorrow night."

He cracked a smile. Barely.

"I meant for the honey-do list."

He raised an eyebrow.

"I have a million things to do tomorrow, but if you could come by in the evening, then I could show you my to-do list, so, you know, you'll be prepared."

"Of course."

"Well ... thank you." She stood awkwardly in front of him.

"Sure thing. See you tomorrow." He spun away and she no longer had to worry about how to end their meeting.

A RAPPING on the door pulled her out of her musings. Seabiscuit's cry became more insistent. She startled and reached for the door, pulling it open without checking to see who was on the other side.

Maybe that's because she already knew.

"'Evenin'."

Rafael stood on the porch, muscular arms crossed, his expression emotionless, if not slightly more relieved looking than it was last night while he stood up on that stage.

She unlatched the screen and swung it open toward him. "Please. Come in."

He ducked into the old house, his frame filling the doorway. She'd never been one to swoon, but she might have to reconsider that. Of course, he wasn't her type, not to mention her family members would all have a hissy fit if she were to look at him for two seconds too long.

She pushed aside any flutterings that tried to take root, knowing they'd be short-lived anyway. He was handsome and all, but she would never do something as dumb as fall in love with him.

Bella was about to invite Rafael into the living room when she realized her siblings were still waiting for her to reappear.

She rose on her tiptoes, cupping her mouth. Tentatively, Rafael bent down to listen to her.

"I'm finishing up a call with my sisters and brother," she whispered to him, the effect more intimate than she would have preferred. "It would be best if you waited in the dining room, okay?"

"Who was that?" Maggie asked when she returned to the call.

Bella shrugged a shoulder. "Just a delivery of something I ordered. Now, about the house—"

"Getting back to Rafael," Lacy cut in, causing the peach fuzz on Bella's arm to stand on end. "He was pretty flaky last month. So he wouldn't have been much help to you anyway. Hate to say it, but I agree with Jakey on this one."

No doubt, Rafael heard that. Bella forced herself not to look at him as he patiently waited for her in the dining room.

"Let's get back to the house update. Or rather, the lack of a house update," Bella said. "Seabiscuit and I are just getting started on the job list—mostly cleaning and fixing small things—so I don't have much of an update yet. Gonna go now. Love you all."

Quickly, Bella disconnected the chat, even as several voices sang out in protest. Hopefully, she hadn't raised anyone's suspicion.

"Sorry about that," she said to Rafael as he stepped forward from the shadows.

"I'm all yours." He didn't attempt to explain why Lacy might have said such a thing about him, or to address the tension in the room, which, she suspected, had something to do with her siblings' feelings for him. Maybe they were mutual.

She spun around, her foot landing haphazardly on Seabiscuit, who yelped appropriately. In one sweeping motion, Rafael bent and picked up the animal, tucked him into the substantial curve of one of his arms, and nodded for Bella to continue.

Didn't she have a to-do list somewhere? Suddenly, she'd lost all recall …

When she didn't speak right away, Rafael smiled kindly. "This place is in nice condition. What is it you need help with?"

She sucked in a breath. "Right! Well, I need switch plates replaced, broken moulding and curtain rods installed, the fireplace cover fixed, so many small things like that." Bella paused, gathering her senses. This was silly. Why was she suddenly so tongue-tied? She stopped, looked at Rafael, and reached out her hands for Seabiscuit.

Her dog came to her, although rather limply, even she had to admit. She rubbed Seabiscuit's noggin. "So can you help me with these things, Rafael?"

"I will not be a flake." He implored her with those dark eyes and that solemn mouth he'd displayed yesterday.

She stared back at him. "I'm sure you won't. Now, my father's old toolbox is in the garage, if you need it."

He smiled at her now. She wanted to believe it was genuine, but her gut—or maybe it was Grace's voice—cautioning her not to be gullible. Maybe Rafael was only placating her, saying what he thought she wanted her to hear.

"I've brought my own tools."

"Great, but I didn't invite you here tonight to work."

"No?"

She shook her head. "I made dinner—gluten-free pasta with my homemade pesto sauce. Thought we could maybe eat and talk over the various jobs. You haven't eaten yet, right?"

Rafael's eyes shifted to her, his brows lowered, as if questioning her sincerity. Did he think she was kidding?

She tilted her head to the side, waiting. "So ... would you like to join me for dinner?"

"Yes, of course. But ..."

"But?"

Rafael leaned on the island, his smile bigger still. "My mother always taught me to bring a hostess gift, and I'm afraid I have not."

"Don't be silly—not that what your mother taught you was silly!" Bella could feel the tension ebbing away as she stepped into the kitchen and set her pup onto the floor to search for scraps. She looked over her shoulder at Rafael. "You're my guest tonight. Can I get you some wine? Water?"

He watched her, and when she continued to stare back at him, he finally said, "Water is good."

She delivered a glass of water to him, with slices of fresh lemon on a small plate. Then she pulled another plate from the cupboard and loaded it up with rice crackers. "I hope you like olives." She opened the fridge. "I made a tapenade earlier to go with those." She set a white ceramic bowl next to the crackers and handed him a spoon.

His smile turned comical. "I thought I was supposed to be your servant for the next week, Bella. Not the other way around."

Bella quirked a smile at him. "You haven't actually seen the honey-do list I've prepared."

"In other words, I should eat up tonight."

"Yes. Gather your strength, my friend." She slid a plate of pasta in front of him and another at her place. "And as my parents would always say, *mangia-mangia*."

He dug into the pasta, savoring its flavor. She could tell by the satisfied look on his face. Bella only used the freshest basil, hand-minced garlic, and her favorite EVOO—extra-virgin olive oil. Her siblings thought she ate twigs and seeds, but if only they'd give her a chance, they would see things differently.

"Bella?"

"Hm?"

"I was sorry to hear about your parents."

Bella nodded. She stepped over to the stove and filled a large bowl with the remaining pasta, bringing it back with her to the table. She didn't like to talk about their passing much, but she appreciated that Rafael acknowledged the elephant in the room. Well, at least one of them. No matter how much she was enjoying her respite at the old beach house, the fact remained that nothing would ever be the same.

She brightened. "So, tell me about you."

His seemingly contented expression ebbed away.

"That bad, huh?"

"That boring."

She laughed lightly. "I doubt that very much."

He finished a bite of pasta. "Because of what Lacy said, you mean?"

Bella shrugged. "My siblings have been babying me my whole life. I love them, but they don't know the grown-up version of me very well."

"How can that be? They're your family."

She smiled and dished him up more pasta. "Eat."

He took another forkful and ate silently for a moment, his gaze growing pensive. Finally, he said, "You remind me of my mother a little."

"She must be very beautiful then."

This coaxed another smile from him. "That is true, yes. Also, very hospitable. Liked to cook for many people at once."

Impulsively, Bella reached over and put her hand on Rafael's arm. She looked straight into his eyes. "That is a very sweet thing to say."

He licked his lips. Then nodded and returned his attention to his meal.

After a quiet minute, and when it looked like they were both about done eating, Bella said, "Would you like me to show you my to-do list now?"

"No."

She frowned.

He flashed her a smile as he slid off the stool. "I'll do the dishes first and then you can show me my tasks for the week."

"Absolutely not!"

"I've got this." He scooped up the plates, took them to the sink, and began rinsing them off.

She watched him working at the sink, the glow of an overhead light illuminating the shifting movements of his shoulder blades beneath his T-shirt. He threw a kitchen towel over one shoulder, like her father always had, and the memory startled her by its sudden appearance, seemingly out of nowhere.

The to-do list could wait. Bella slid back onto a stool at the island and began drumming her fingers on the countertop, watching him. "Are you one of those guys who pre-washes every dish before putting it into the dishwasher?"

His hands slowed, but he didn't turn around. "The manual says it's best to rinse dishes beforehand." His voice held a tinge of a smile.

"Rinse, yes. But you're over there scrubbing like those dishes have been outside all day playing in the mud."

Rafael pulled the towel from his shoulder and turned quickly, flicking it at her.

Bella squealed and shrank back.

His lips were turned up into a quirky smile as he stared her down and slowly flopped that towel back over his shoulder.

She saluted him. "Message received."

He chuckled. "Let that be a lesson to you."

"Okay. Lesson number one—do not criticize Rafael's dishwashing regimen."

He shook water droplets from a plate before putting it inside the dishwasher. "I'll have you know this regimen, as you call it, served my family well for more than thirty years."

"Wow. That's a long time. I'm guessing you've been washing dishes since you were a toddler."

"My mother was a taskmaster."

"Then I salute her too."

Dishes done, he turned around and braced his hands on the counter behind him. "Ready."

Bella took in Rafael standing there in her family's kitchen, all six-foot-something of him. With that spotlight over his waves of dark hair, highlighting the strength in his shoulders, she clearly saw the reason for his fame in town. But she didn't see the bad boy part. Not really.

For the past hour or so, Rafael had been nothing but friendly. Charming, even. And helpful. If she were ready to put down roots, he might have been perfect, but as her life stood now, Bella was just passing through.

"Perfect," she said, exhaling. "Let's get started."

RAFAEL HAD NEVER BEEN SO STARSTRUCK in his life. Not even when he bumped into LeAnn Rimes at the county fair and nearly splashed her with beer after carrying two overpriced cups of the stuff for him and his date.

Get it together, man.

He usually didn't talk to himself, either. Not unless there was a good reason, like an angelic woman paying good money for him—money that would go to a charity to help little bitty animals.

Rafael pictured Bella's expression after she'd bailed him out of the bachelor lineup, explaining how she did not expect—nor want—a week of dates. Instead, could he help her with chores around the house?

He chuckled just thinking about it. She didn't slip her arm into his and flaunt their newly formed bond in front of the other bidders. Or try to lure him into her bedroom soon after—in fact, she'd told him she didn't want to see his mug for another twenty-four hours. She even agreed to give him plenty of days off, which stretched his commitment over several weeks instead of one. And something else she didn't do was haul him in front of the camera when her siblings were talking trash about him on their conference call.

Oh, and she made him dinner.

Morning had come and he found himself back there first thing, working away on minor repairs. He hummed softly as he removed the window blinds from their brackets and began untangling cords from where they had gotten hung up on a spool. The blinds weren't all that old, but they had become dried and stuck from the salt in the air. From what tidbits he'd heard about the situation, the family could not spend very much on their repairs—a requirement in their parents' will. When he spotted Bella wrestling with these blinds this morning, he couldn't help but swoop in and take the task from her.

She seemed pleased. Had sighed a little sigh, touched his arm, and headed back down the hall to do who-knew-what. He had not been able to chase away the image of her reaction to him ever since.

The sound of the house's front door opening, followed by female voices, slowed him, bringing him to the present. If he weren't mistaken, Bella's oldest sister Maggie had just arrived.

He scratched his chin with the back of two fingers. He and Maggie had been friends once—she'd seemed to acknowledge that fact when she first arrived in Colibri a few months ago. But that new husband of hers, Luke, the town's surfer boy, always seemed to have a chip on his shoulder whenever Rafael would dare to walk the same path as he did. Didn't know what the guy's problem was. Frankly, didn't care too much about it either.

Bella appeared in the doorway. "Hey, Rafael, my sister, Mags, is here."

"Maggie." He nodded quickly and returned to his work.

"Hey, Rafael." She stood quietly for a moment, apprising him. "You're a lucky man."

He waited, listening for more.

She continued, "My sister's the sweetest boss you could ask for."

He turned to look at her more fully. Her expression wore a warning, her eyebrows frozen upward, and he could guess her meaning: *Touch my sister and you die.*

Rafael gave Bella a small smile. "I agree with you there,

Maggie. Although the honey-do list she gave me last night might take more than seven days to accomplish."

Maggie dug her fist into her waist, her other hand holding a paper bag. "It better not." She swung a look at Bella. "I'll keep your secret safe for now, but I can't hold off our brother forever."

Bella laughed lightly and waved her sister off like she was being silly. "I'm not worried about him, but"—she cast a glance at Rafael now, her eyes wide, her expression thoughtful—"if I'm overworking you, Rafael, I mean, if I'm asking too much—"

He chuckled. "Not at all, Bella. I was teasing you." He shot a harder look at Maggie, hoping she'd get his meaning, i.e., *You and your siblings don't scare me.*

Maggie sighed and dropped her hand to her side. "I'll leave you to your work. I've got something to talk to Bella about now." She shook the paper bag she'd been holding in front of her little sister's face. "I brought you some muffin tops."

"Muffin ... tops? Oh yummy. Those are the best part!"

Maggie laughed and cast one more look at Rafael before following Bella down the hall.

He returned to his work, his senses on alert. Even as he continued the tedious job of unraveling all that tangled-up cord, he could hear them carrying on. They were talking about him, voices low, but recognizable just the same. He stilled, listening, knowing he shouldn't but unable to help himself.

Bella's voice began. "Thanks so—"

"Seriously, what is he doing here, Bella?" Maggie's voice, though hushed, came through loud and clear.

Bella shushed her, the tone of her voice a desperate whisper. "I told you all last night. I bought Rafael's services at the bachelor auction. He's mine for a week's worth of work and Jake has nothing to say about it."

"Oh he has something to say about it, all right."

"But do you?"

"Do I ... what?"

"Mags, I thought you kinda liked him. I mean, not in a romantic way—everybody knows you've been in love with Luke for ages. But, I don't know, I guess I thought that maybe you guys had some kind of friendship, at least when you were a kid."

Rafael didn't hear Maggie's answer, but frankly, he thought so too. He glanced out the bedroom window, remembering one night in particular, years ago, when he and Maggie had curled up in one another's arms right out on that big beach for the night. Nothing inappropriate had happened. She was in tears, and he had enough sense not to take advantage of that.

By the next morning, though, the town gossip chain had been activated. Maggie left town, and that was that. He furrowed his brow, remembering. Maybe he should have done more to stop the tongues from flapping from ear to ear. But he was young, and though he could hardly recall his thoughts from the morning after that night, if he were to guess, he probably had no intention of stopping any such mouth flapping.

Rafael's heart sank a little lower in his chest. He was *that* guy—the one who willingly let rumors multiply as long as they made him look good. At least to his mind. Never really mattered who else might get hurt along the way, or, at least he doesn't recall thinking too much about all that. Truth was, those rumors about him were far more exciting than his real life.

A droplet of sweat skittered down his cheek and onto his chin. Rafael wiped it away with the back of his hand, realization causing him to perspire more. He had no designs on Bella. She was much younger than him. Too delicate to mishandle. Simply put, he was not good enough for her.

Rafael released a long slow breath, clearing his mind as best he could. He must stick with his plan, and that was to continue to take the job he'd been offered. To work hard and pay off his mother's debts. And to eventually buy himself a place with room to expand, far, far away from here.

He glanced out that window again, the sea churning and unsettled. Even if Bella would have him, he wouldn't be around long, nor would he be falling for a Holloway girl anytime soon.

"Rafael?"

He jerked his gaze toward the doorway where Bella stood, watching him quizzically.

"You were staring into space."

"Sorry." He vaguely remembered the sound of the front door closing.

She stepped into the room, her relaxed smile gone, and he girded himself for a proper ousting. No doubt big sister Maggie gave Bella a talking-to and she was about to boot him out of their house. It didn't matter anyway. He still had plenty to do at home, projects that would move him closer to his goal of getting out of this town, this state, for good. He could use the extra time anyway.

"I need your help."

He narrowed his eyes. If he weren't mistaken, tears threatened to let loose from behind those lovely eyes. She did not sound like a woman who was about to send him away.

"Anything, Bella. What is it?"

She sighed and entered the room fully now, lowering herself to the bed with that faded old fish on it. "The shelter is being forced to close."

"The ten grand they raised wasn't enough?"

"Not to Lillian Madsen. That's why Maggie was here, to tell me that Ms. Madsen sent word to the shelter already that she plans to go ahead with evicting all those poor little animals."

"You're kidding." He slid the blinds header back in its bracket with more force than probably necessary. "Are they that far behind in rent?"

"No, they're not. The money raised from the auction caught them all up, but I guess there's some provision in the lease that says she can kick them out anyway." She crossed her arms, her eyes downcast. "Doesn't seem fair."

He wagged his head slowly. Lillian Madsen was no friend of his and this latest move of hers did not surprise him at all.

Bella shifted. "Maybe I should talk to Grace about this. Not sure if you remember her, but she and her husband are both lawyers."

"I remember Grace." He paused, not sure if he should be the one to relay the futility of fighting Lillian Madsen. "You could definitely try."

"Then again, maybe it's too late. Maggie says Ms. Madsen has plans to tear down several of her buildings to build a super center. Can you see some big box store on Colibri's main street? Seems to me that it would ruin the whole feel of it around here." She sighed again, the sound of it like feathers in a soft breeze, and he wanted to run right out of there. "So," she said, "will you help me?"

Tension knotted Rafael's forehead.

"I mean, we can't let this happen, Rafael. Maybe Ms. Madsen has a legal right to retake her building from the shelter, but someone needs to help all those critters find a new home." She looked up at him, her eyes wide and penetrating. "Maybe you and I can put our heads together and figure out how to help. I mean, you obviously love the place, or you wouldn't have volunteered to be auctioned off. Right?"

Volunteered? Hardly. He'd been roped into it, cattle prodded, so to speak, by his brother's old girlfriend, Clementine, who ran the place. She'd begged him. Stroked his ego, telling him the shelter would get a high price for him. His reputation had taken a beating recently, especially while his mother was sick. Everyone around here seemed to think he was a ... leech.

So he had agreed. For as much as his mother's reputation as his own.

His gaze moved over Bella's hopeful expression. In it he saw open-faced trust that he couldn't fathom. Rafael swallowed the sigh that tried to push itself out of him. He had things to do, a life to run after, but how could he resist that sweet face staring up at him?

The truth was, he couldn't.

3

———

Bella glanced over at Rafael, who was in the driver's seat of his truck, an intense expression stuck on his face.

He swiveled a look at her. "What?"

"Nothing."

Rafael turned his eyes back to the road. "Didn't look like nothing."

She shifted her body to face him. "Just wondering where your hat is."

"Hat?"

"The first time I saw you—that day while you were gardening—you were wearing a cowboy hat, and I thought it suited you."

A smile broke through his expression. "Is that right?"

"Oh yes. That and the way you hum."

"Hum?"

"Noticed it when you're working." She crossed her arms casually and sat back. "Anyway, there's something earnest about a man working in the sun, shading his tan face with the wide brim of a cowboy hat."

"Sounds like a novel or something."

"What's wrong with that?"

He shrugged. "Nothing, I guess. As long as it doesn't cause one to believe that one of those stories could happen in real life."

"Oh? And what would happen if *one* did dare to believe in a happy ending?"

He waved a hand in the air haphazardly and let it flop back onto the steering well. "All this from a hat, huh?"

"Did somebody break your heart, Rafael?"

He sputtered. "Whoa, that was from nowhere. What does that mean?"

"I've been trying to figure out what's behind those pensive looks of yours and it just came to me that maybe it's about a girl. There are a lot of songs written about broken hearts, you know."

Rafael considered her, his mouth a questioning smile. He turned his gaze back to the road. "There's no girl."

"Well, if there *was* a girl, I'm sure she would love to see you in that hat."

He laughed, the sound of it filling the truck cab. "Bella, I—"

A text lit up her phone. Kyle. She bit the inside of her cheek and braved a look at what he had to say.

"You okay?"

Bella jerked her chin up to find Rafael's concerned expression trained on her. "Sorry?"

"I was just about to tease you about your cowboy hat fetish, but—"

"Oh my gosh, Rafael, it's not a fetish!" She shoved her phone into her pocket. "You are seriously handsome in that hat, and I decided it would be nice to give you a compliment."

She paused, realizing her knee-jerk reaction might have more to do with her text from Kyle than it did with Rafael's good-natured teasing. "Well, anyway, just thought it might be something worth hearing right now. That's all."

"Worth hearing right now? You mean in my currently pensive state?"

"Yes."

He hummed softly, a grin on his face.

"There it is again. My momma always hummed too. I think she always had some melody playing in her head."

"And you think I do as well?"

Bella cast a look at him. "For what it's worth, yes, I do."

He felt the heat rising in his skin. He cleared his throat. "Daisy didn't like it all that much."

"Daisy?"

"I did some work around her place, pre-Jake, and, well, I caught her batting the air once when I was humming. I didn't realize it, of course. Not until she was swatting the air like some kind of June Bug was flying around her head. Guess my humming sounded like some awful buzzing."

"That's funny."

"Yeah. Real hilarious."

Bella rested her head on the seat back, smiling. "Well, I like the sound of it. You have a nice voice, Rafael."

"You're very kind."

"What is the song that you are ... humming?"

He returned her gaze with a quizzical look. "I'm not sure that I know."

"It's quite beautiful."

He licked his lips. "I believe it's something my mother played on her guitar. Hadn't thought about that in a long while."

"That's sweet. I've always wanted to learn to play the guitar." She sighed, looking off into the distance. "And I understand how things remind us of our mamas unexpectedly."

This time he gave her a grim look.

"It's okay. I've made my peace with things—they taught me well."

He only nodded.

"You know, my parents were quite old when they had me —I'm thankful they didn't quit with four."

"Four?"

"Kids." She laughed. "I had the luxury of being the baby of the family."

"And you lapped it up?"

"Didn't know that's what I was doing, but yes, I guess so. Except ..."

When her words trailed off, he glanced at her, his gaze prodding.

"They all still treat me like a baby." Bella stuck her tongue out then immediately retracted it. "Guess that wasn't the best reaction."

Rafael laughed. "I won't tell. Being the baby of the family isn't something I can relate to, but I will say that being the oldest comes with built-in concerns for the rest of the family."

"In other words, don't be so hard on my siblings."

"If they deserve it, go for it. But ..."

"But?"

He dipped his head in her direction and gave her a quick look. "Maybe hear them out and cut 'em some slack if what they say comes from the heart and not just a thick head."

"You mean like what some of them said about me hiring you?"

He didn't respond.

"I know you heard them, Rafael. Was nice of you to act otherwise, but I know it hurt your feelings."

Rafael kept his eyes on the road. "I can take it."

She considered him. Bella wasn't stupid. She recognized why so many were hootin' and hollerin' the other night when he strutted across that stage at the auction. And though she was younger than the rest of her sisters, she vaguely remembered the girls and their friends talking about him on the beach. Apparently, he didn't wear a shirt all that much—though she'd yet to see that.

There was something wounded about him, though, a downcast look in his eyes that niggled at her heart. Bella didn't know what to make of it exactly, but somehow she wished she could apply a tourniquet and see that he was healed up properly before she said goodbye to Colibri for good.

Before she could continue this conversation, they arrived at the shelter.

Rafael looked through the truck's windshield. "Know what you're going to do when Clementine tells you it's true?"

"It'll come to me. I'm sure." She unlatched the door. "At least we can give those poor deserted animals some love."

Rafael hopped out of the truck and came around to Bella's side where he held the door open for her. She nodded her appreciation and landed, boots first, on the crumbling pavement. Even from here, they could hear the barks, yaps, and occasional whines coming from inside the shelter.

Clementine's ponytail was particularly severe today. "Hey," she said, barely looking up when they wandered in.

Rafael reached over the counter and gave Clementine's shoulder a quick rub. "We heard the news. You doing okay?"

"Not really." She snapped a look toward the door leading to where the animals were kept safe. "She sure didn't give us much time to find homes for all those animals."

"May we see them?" Bella asked.

"Sure." Clementine opened the gate for them, her body language reflecting her melancholy. "There's hand sanitizer by the exit. Take your time."

The cement floors and walls did little to mask the sounds of dogs and other animals looking for some love. A few young volunteers wearing bright T-shirts milled about, some feeding the animals, others going to or from walks. Two in particular sat on the floor in cages, petting and talking softly to the animals.

Bella's heart clenched and tears pushed against the backs of her eyes. Seeing so many homeless animals reminded her of the first time she'd spotted Seabiscuit as he waited to be adopted.

Rafael stopped and reached in to let a German Shepherd smell his hand. He gave the animal a pet and chucked him under the chin.

"How can you do that without breaking down?"

"Because I know Clementine and this guy here'll find an owner eventually. This is a no-kill shelter, you know."

"Yes, I know. But she's going to have to work fast if another suitable home isn't found quickly."

Rafael nodded, his expression sober. "It's pretty cramped in here. Maybe it would be better for the shelter to move on."

"Silver lining?"

"Something like that."

"Just like I thought ... under all that gruffness lives a soft spot."

Rafael twisted a hard gaze at her. "Gruffness? Me?"

She laughed. "You old softie."

"Come on." Rafael grabbed her hand and began pulling her down the aisle, their boots smacking against the cement floors.

"Where are we going?"

"You'll see."

They turned a corner, past more doggies in crates, and through a doorway that led outside. Bella gasped. In front of them lay a pen filled with hay bales and ... goats. Lots and lots of baby goats.

She put a hand to her heart. "Oh ... my ... word."

Rafael leaned against the walls, arms crossed. "Thought you might find them interesting."

Bella approached the pen, swung the gate open, and squealed. She cast a smile and a glance over her shoulder at Rafael who slipped in behind her and quickly shut the gate.

On her hands and knees, Bella laughed as goat after goat snuggled up to her, bleating its welcome. She rolled onto her behind and crossed her legs, not having to coax any of them to join her.

"Wow. You really are a goat whisperer."

Bella smiled up at him. "They just love the attention."

"Nuh-uh. I think they love you." He unfolded his arms and squatted down on his haunches to pet one of the larger goats.

"I wonder if any of these goats have ever done yoga."

"What?!" Rafael snapped wide eyes at her.

"Sorry. Thinking out loud. I was just remembering the goat yoga I did a few times up in Washington."

Rafael stared at her like she spoke a foreign language, which, to him, might have been the case.

Bella twisted a questioning look at him. "Does that look mean you've never heard of it or you've never tried it?"

"I think you're making it up."

Bella laughed lightly as a baby goat pounced into her lap and offered her chin a kiss. He smelled like hay and the outdoors. "It's not new, you know."

"Is to me."

"Well, then maybe we'll just have to get you signed up for a class."

He whistled and shook his head. "Good luck, darlin'."

Bella leaned her head to one side, watching him.

"What?"

"Nothing. I was just imagining you saying that with your cowboy hat on." When his already-tan dark skin colored some, she looked away. She wasn't flirting—had it looked like that? Oh brother. See? She never was good at all that; reading male signals was an art she had never mastered.

If she'd been better at that, maybe she wouldn't have found herself in a relationship with Kyle. She worked at the reference desk of the library part-time, and he came in asking for the Wi-Fi password. When he'd asked for her number—in case he had trouble logging on—she figured, why not? How was she to know he wanted more than internet access?

"I suppose you might find out sometime."

Bella scrunched her eyes, focusing on Rafael. "Sorry? I missed that."

He cracked a smile. "I think all those goats have got you preoccupied."

"Maybe." Suddenly, she couldn't think of a word to say. She was sitting in a pen filled with goats and her, er, handy-man, aka bachelor, looking on. Her face flushed—she could feel it. Bella began to stand, not wanting to lead Rafael on about anything ...

"Too bad you can't take some of them home with you," he said.

One of the goats peered into her face, as if pleading for her to do just that. She swallowed back a reply, frozen in place. What if ... what if she could take some of them with her?

She darted a look up at Rafael, a dream of a plan taking shape.

"Unless, of course, you *want* to take one with you." He laughed as if that were absurd.

"Maybe I do."

Rafael stilled.

She stood and laughed and grabbed hold of his arms. "So gullible you are. I've got work to do and, sadly, can't take one of these cuties with me. But—"

"But?"

"I was thinking."

"Really."

She surveyed the goat pen, one hand digging into her hip now. "This pen—this place—is not suitable for these animals, even if they were to get a reprieve from Ms. Madsen."

"Which, I'm sure, they won't."

She nodded. "Right. What about an animal sanctuary? Is there one around here?"

"You mean a place for larger animals? A place on open land? No." He shook his head. "Not that I know of."

"Well, there should be."

Rafael released a breath at the same time that he rubbed the back of his neck, his eyes training a wary gaze on her.

"I suppose it'll take a little more time than I have." She gave the goats a lingering glance. "But I sure would like to see these animals housed in a better place."

Rafael stepped forward, squatting down until his eyes were level with hers. In them she saw kindness. And empathy. She had no idea why her siblings found fault with this kind man ...

"Bella!"

Rafael swiveled, still close to the ground. Bella peered around him.

Maggie stood outside of the pen, a motherly scowl on her face.

"Hey."

Maggie shook her head slowly, her eyes steady on Bella's. "Seriously, girl, are you getting anything done in the house?"

Bella swallowed back her response. She slid a look at Rafael, wondering what he thought about her big sister's sudden appearance. For her, Maggie's attitude toward her was as natural as brushing her teeth in the morning, though why it should be at her age, she couldn't say.

Bella stood, dusting straw from her pants. "Don't worry, Mags. We've been working all morning and just decided to take a break and see what was happening here."

Maggie frowned, her eyes trained on Bella. She spoke with a lowered voice. "I heard today that Lillian tried to pull a fast one with the city council and get a rubber stamp on a zoning change."

"How'd you hear that?"

Maggie flashed her brows. "I've got a friend in the know, Bella Boo."

"You mean Luke." She lowered her voice. "And I would prefer if you wouldn't call me that. I'm an adult now, after all."

Maggie sighed. She broke eye contact and looked around the pen. "They are cute little buggers."

Bella walked toward her, the spell of the past few minutes broken. "Yup. They are. Kind of wish I could take some home with me."

Maggie threw an arm around Bella as she exited the pen, Rafael on their heels. "This does not surprise me." She kissed her temple, the sound of it like a soft smack. "Promise me you'll stay on the house project, okay? We're under a deadline and I know how easily you become distracted."

Bella noticed Maggie's almost-imperceptible glance back at Rafael when she said that. She shook free of her sister. "Thanks. I will."

Maggie continued to hover near Rafael and Bella even after they wandered outside and toward the truck. Finally, Rafael turned to Bella. "Ready to go?"

"If you need a ride, Bella," Maggie cut in, "I could drive you."

Bella shrugged. "No thanks. Rafael and I have one more errand to run before we go back to the house to work on projects."

Rafael opened the door for Bella, and she climbed into his truck. As Bella waved at Maggie, she couldn't help but notice the deflated expression on her big sister's face.

To Rafael, Maggie had always seemed like a strong-willed woman, motherly almost. So it should not have been a surprise to him that she would show up and question Bella about her detour to the shelter. She hadn't been unkind, rather, she seemed ... curious. Maybe fretful.

He thought about this as he and Bella made their way out of town and back to the beach house. He had seen a look like the one Maggie wore on her face before, from his own mother. And it drove him. At least, now it did. He couldn't very well say that had always been the case.

Rafael glanced at Bella, who was unusually quiet. "You okay?"

"Hm?" She turned to him with questioning wide eyes.

"You are being very quiet."

"I'm thinking." She swiveled in her seat and tilted her gaze up at him. "Would you mind taking a drive with me?"

Rafael paused, Maggie's motherly threat still ringing in his mind.

Bella continued. "I mean, unless I'm taking advantage of

your time. I mean, I know I bought you to work on the house and all, and this is a kind of detour."

He laughed. "Another one."

"Yes. Another one."

"I don't mind, Bella. Where do you want to go?"

She inhaled, her gaze intense, like she was trying to figure out just that. "I'm trying to remember exactly how to get there." She tapped her chin. "I think it's up that twisty hill. It's this property with burnt-out steps and no house on it."

Punch to the gut. That was the best way to describe how Rafael felt when Bella mentioned the land that had once belonged to his father.

Involuntarily, he exhaled, the sound of it like a groan.

"Turn around."

"Excuse me?"

She was sitting up stick straight right now, worry etching her features. "Turn around, Rafael. We don't need to do this right now."

He slowed the truck but didn't turn. "Have you changed your mind? You seemed awfully sure of it back there."

"I'm sure. I've taken up too much of your time."

He pulled the truck to the side of the road and stared at her. Tears were pricking her eyes. Where did those come from?

She peered at him. "I feel I have put you in a difficult situation. Sometimes ... sometimes I get an idea in my head and find myself just going forward with it. I'm trying to learn that not everyone shares my enthusiasm for certain things."

Despite the weird headspace he had found himself in a

moment before, he grinned at her. "Are those Maggie's words or your own?"

She scrunched her eyes. "I don't know what you mean."

Rafael put the truck in park and turned to her, one hand behind her seat rest. "Here is how I see it. You asked me to drive you somewhere but saw the look on my face and thought your request bothered me. Is that right?"

"Yes, but—"

"But it's not true. Sorry, but that's the truth. You asking me to drive you to that overgrown lot on the hill and my response has nothing to do with you." He swallowed a moment, considering her. She had not taken her eyes from his face, as if she were actually listening to what he was saying. Such a novelty. Rafael cleared his throat. "Now, do you still want to go see it?"

She stuck her tongue to her upper lip and nodded. For some reason he couldn't figure out, that made him smile. So what if she wanted to see the glimpse of his father's past? She didn't need to know that's how he thought of it.

"Okay, then. Let's go." Rafael put the truck in gear and released the brake. Minutes later, they reached the spot that he saw mostly in pictures in his mind. He pushed those thoughts away and hopped out of the truck. Might as well find out what's so fascinating to Bella.

Her face lit up as they climbed the stairs to nowhere.

He frowned. "Owner needs to clear the land."

Bella pivoted, her smile brighter than ever. "Do they ever."

"What's got you so happy about that?"

She shrugged happily. "Let's go look around. C'mon."

He followed her to the top of the steps and onto the

dusty lot with its peek-a-boo ocean view and spattering of pines. Bella sighed, the sound of it like playful kittens. He was beginning to question how long he could manage to ignore how lovable she was.

She grabbed him by the arm and pulled him farther down the center of the property. "I want to see how far back this goes. Hopefully we won't get into trouble or anything."

"Yeah, that could go very badly for me."

Bella sent him a worried glance.

"Your brother'll bail you out and leave me stewing in the jailhouse."

She cracked a smile, followed by peals of light laughter. Then she skipped on ahead like a pre-teen on an adventure. At one point, Bella stopped and looked up, bracing her hands on her back for balance.

"Look at all that sky up there," she said.

He quirked a look upward. Yeah, there was sky all right.

She continued, walking toward the edge of the lot on the west side. He followed behind and reached out a hand to steady her, though she didn't really seem to need it. Then again, did she realize how sheer that cliff was?

"Well?" he finally said in the silence. "Did you find what you were looking for?"

She tilted a look back at him. "You don't happen to know who owns this lot, do you?"

Was that a trick question?

"It's okay if you don't. I was just musing." She sighed in that way of hers again.

Rafael stuck his hand in his back pocket and looked out toward the ocean. He took it all in— the blue, the rolls of white foam, the horizon that stretched beyond what the eye could see. It had always been there for him, like flip-flops on the porch and beers around the fire after the sun had set for the evening.

For the first time he wondered: Would he miss it? Or would he walk away from this place and embrace the invigoration of starting over? Rafael glanced toward Bella and startled. She was looking straight at him.

"One thing's for sure," she said. "If I owned this place, I'd get it cleared ASAP before the fire department sent out a warning."

He slid a glance to the overgrowth everywhere. "They probably already have. It's easy to do, but time consuming. Not to mention dirty, sweaty work."

"Not if you're a goat."

"Come again?"

"I feel bad for all those goats at the shelter."

"The ones all penned up?"

Bella gasped. "Rafael! You're funny."

"Occasionally." He shrugged.

"Goats love weeds. Trust me on this. What I was thinking is that we could bring all those goats up here and clear this land super fast."

"We?" He narrowed his eyes, trying not to laugh.

Bella's face reddened slightly, and guilt pecked at him. "Or you could maybe loan me your truck?"

Rafael laughed heartily now, grateful for the sensation of laughter rolling out of him. He hadn't wanted to get involved in whatever was going on with the shelter, or with the Holloways, especially since none of the guys in the family seemed to like him all that much.

But Bella Holloway was making his distaste for the lot of

them hard to hang onto. She watched him expectantly, her eyes trained on him, her lips parted slightly. How in the world could he say no to that?

He looked her in the eyes. "If that's something you decide to propose to the animal shelter this week, then I will help you."

"Actually," Bella said, taking his arm, "I was thinking that this property would be a great place to build an animal sanctuary. I mean, look how deep it goes!"

"Do you always have such wild ideas?"

Bella quieted and her animated expression faded away. She let go of his arm and broke eye contact with him. "Maybe you're right."

"About?"

She was quiet a moment. "I really should be getting back to the house now. My list of things to do isn't getting any shorter, is it?"

Bella turned back the way they came, but Rafael reached out and touched her shoulder. When she stopped, he gently turned her around to face him. "What's bothering you?"

"Oh don't worry about me, Rafael. I'm a big girl, although ..." She waved him away and attempted a smile he didn't buy.

"What were you going to say?"

Bella sighed, an uncomfortable look on her face, and slid a glance up at him. "My family thinks I'm a flake. They always have." She began playing with her hair, pulling it into a ponytail and then dropping it back to her shoulders. "The curse of being the youngest, I suppose."

He didn't answer her right away, instead feeling appropriately sorry for his part in reminding her of sad memories. "Guess I could say the same."

"What do you mean? Are you the youngest?"

"No. But my brother wasn't in my life at first—he's a half-brother." He paused, not wishing to explain. He continued. "So for some time, I was the only one."

"And your family thinks you're a ... oh."

At the look of sudden realization on her pretty face, Rafael broke out a brief laugh. "Like your family does."

"They are harmless."

He nodded. "I'm sure, but admittedly, I missed an appointment with Lacy last month. I was supposed to help her out in the house, but I was"—he paused, considering his words—"delayed. In the end, I was unable to make it at all."

"Well, sometimes I think Lacy's memory is better than Maggie's."

Rafael laughed at this. For someone so kind and easygoing, her sense of humor surprised him with their sneak attacks. How long had it been since he had laughed so many times in one day?

His smile faded as he stole a glance at her and saw regret on her face. "I don't think you're a flake."

She paused a moment before saying, "I don't think you are either."

"Can't say that you'd be right."

"Oh no? How many flakes let themselves be ogled by women for a good cause?"

Was he supposed to answer that?

"You showed up, so in my mind, you're not flaky at all." She smiled. "Thanks for giving me a pep talk. I guess being here brought back old memories or something. Speaking of which ..."

Once again, her voice trailed off as if she'd become distracted by a sudden thought. He noted the telltale sign of laser-like attention focused somewhere in the distance.

"What is it?"

"I guess I didn't realize how much of the beach could be seen from up here. Thought we were too low." She turned to him. "Lacy's property has a great view, but this one's not bad either. Especially with those Topa Topa Mountains in the distance on the other side."

He knew this, though he wasn't about to tell her why. Or anyone.

She continued. "You know, there's something I've always wanted to do."

Rafael waited.

She peered up at him. "Have you ever ridden a horse on the beach?"

"Nope." He shoved his hands into his back pockets, hard. "Can't say that I have."

"I've always wanted to. Look at how that soft sand goes on for miles. I bet that would be amazing." She sighed that feathery sigh that was getting under his skin. "I wonder if it's allowed here?"

Rafael held his tongue for a good long while. Finally, he said, "Can't say I've ever seen anyone ridin' one on the beach." He didn't mention that horses were housed not too far from here in the shadow of those Topa Topas, that he could drive up a dusty road, deeper into the hills, and see any number of them. Telling her so would lead to more questions, and that's a box Rafael didn't care to open right now. Or ever.

"Hm. Well, maybe someday." She smiled at him. "Want to go back and help me with my to-do list?"

"Like I have a choice?"

For a quick second, Bella's expression fell. She laughed then and punched his arm before starting for the steps that led to the street. "You are my servant for the time being, you know."

"Oh I know!" He grinned and sidestepped around her, holding out his hand when she reached the top step.

She put her hand in his. "Such service."

4

———

The next morning Bella walked down to the bakery with Seabiscuit and stopped to let the pup lap up some water from the bowl Brooke left out for canine friends. She connected his leash to the hook outside and wandered in.

Brooke greeted her with a smile and a smudge of white flour on her cheek.

"Good morning, Bella."

"Good morning to you too, Brooke. You look like you've been here awhile already."

"Yes, ma'am. That would be every morning!"

Bella inhaled the aromas of sugar and yeast that permeated the bakery. She perused the glass case. "Everything looks so fresh."

"That's because it is. And made with love, of course."

"Aw, I love that so much. I'll take one of everything then," she quipped.

Brooke grinned. "Coffee, too?"

"Please. And seriously, I'd love two lemon muffin tops."

"Of course. Will someone be joining you?"

Bella shook her head. "I'm just hungry."

"Sure thing." Brooke laughed. "Find a seat and I'll bring your breakfast out to you."

Bella settled into a spot near the window where she could keep an eye on Seabiscuit, who had, thankfully, curled into a ball and fallen asleep. She didn't drink coffee as religiously as her siblings did—tea was more of her preference—but this morning she woke up dragging a little. She and Rafael had worked late into the evening, she wiping down missed spots on the woodwork and he cleaning window rails all over the house. They'd ordered a veggie pizza from Matty's and sat at the island talking and eating until late, as if they'd been friends forever.

Brooke appeared with a hot cup of coffee, a plate of muffin tops, and whipped butter. "You look lost in thought this morning."

"Do I?"

"Maybe you just need a little caffeine to get you going."

Bella took the coffee but didn't take a sip. "Can I ask you a question?"

"Anything."

"What do you know about Rafael?"

Brooke's smile was slow and tinged with a secret sort of mirth. "Well ..."

"I mean, what do you *really* know? Not, like, what have you *heard*?"

"Hm. Thanks for clarifying." She put her thumb and forefinger under her chin, as if supporting it as she thought.

"I know that he's, well, he's a handsome guy. Seems to be quite fit. And has free time on his hands ..."

Bella frowned.

Brooke glanced around the empty shop and then pulled out a chair and sat across from Bella. "Are you interested in him, honey?"

Bella shook her head. "No, no, nothing like that."

"Okay, all right." Brooke's eyes watched her kindly. "I didn't mean to imply anything. The truth is, I don't know Rafael all that much. He came in a lot when we first opened and, hm ..."

"What?"

Brooke tilted her head and looked at Bella, a sobering look in her eyes. "He used to pick up one eclair. I think it was for his mother, actually. He hasn't done that in weeks."

"That's so sweet. He mentioned her to me once."

"Yes. Hopefully she's feeling okay. Maybe I should ask him next time he's in." The bell rang on the front door and Brooke automatically slid out of her seat. "You know what? I bet she just got tired of all those eclairs!"

"Impossible!"

"I know, right?" Brooke winked and scampered off to help her next customer.

After Brooke dashed away, Bella glanced out the window to see Seabiscuit opening his eyes. In them she saw a silent plea to take him home. Quickly, she drank her coffee and ate one of the muffin tops. She folded a napkin around the other one and tucked it into her jacket pocket for the walk.

When she arrived back home, Rafael was waiting for her on the porch wearing that old hat she'd first seen on him. She tried not to stare.

"Thought I told you to sleep in," she said, climbing the wooden steps. She reached into her pocket and pulled out breakfast. "Here. I brought you a muffin top."

He smiled and took it from her. "Did you eat the bottom?"

"Don't tell me you've never partaken of one of Brooke's amazing muffin tops before! I mean, I know I'm new around here, but even I know all about their magic."

"Magic, huh?" Rafael plucked the lemony goodness from the bag and took a big bite. He nodded and licked his lips. "Pretty magical."

Bella rolled her eyes and stepped up to the door, careful not to let her eyes linger on Rafael as she passed him on the porch. Seabiscuit bounded into the house in front of her. "You are a glutton for punishment, aren't you? Well, come on in now."

She led him inside and stopped.

Rafael pulled up right behind her, and Bella could feel his warm breath on her neck. It wasn't unwelcome. "What is it?"

She shook off her musings, poked a fist into her waist, and called out behind her. "It's that couch. You know, my family has already changed so many things that I would not have—the kitchen, for example—oh, but that couch." She wrinkled her nose and threw a glance at Rafael over her shoulder. "It really is past its time."

"You're not a fan of insect parts and dead sand fleas?"

Bella peeled a look over her shoulder at him and he flashed her a grin.

"Nothing that a vacuum couldn't suck up," he said.

"Gross."

"I've got another idea."

"Hopefully one less graphic."

He continued. "I'll haul that rat bag out of here for you and replace it with one my brother Serge just cleaned. You know that he has his own carpet cleaning business, yes?"

"I did not know that."

"It's true."

She glanced at the old couch, a sudden melancholy coming over her.

Rafael shifted, concern etched in his expression. "You good with this?"

Bella looked from Rafael to the ratty old couch that, for some reason, none of her siblings had been able to part with. Even she was having second thoughts. "You think it'll fit okay?"

He surveyed the room, seeming to measure it with his gaze. "Yes. It's large and in much better shape than that one. Do you like blue?"

"Much more than dingy brown, yes. But ..."

He stared at her, expectantly.

"I have a pretty strict budget. Can you get me a good price?"

Rafael retreated outside but called to her over his shoulder. "I can. Give me a little time and I'll bring Serge with me to move that old one and haul it away for you."

She leaned out the door. "But I could help."

"I'm sure you could, but no." Rafael tilted his hat back, which sent a warm little wave through her. "I'll get my brother to help. Be back in a few minutes, Bella."

She watched him climb into his truck and pull out of the driveway like a man with a mission in mind.

Seabiscuit thumped his tail repeatedly, as if suddenly thrilled to have Bella all to himself again.

Bella patted his noggin. "You ate a big breakfast, my friend. But I guess I could find you a snack." She fetched a bag of sweet potato jerky and plopped down onto the kitchen floor, cross-legged. Seabiscuit did that thing he always did when excited—lowered onto his haunches, tail wagging in the air. Bella covered the snack with her hand.

"Wait for it."

The dog let out a squeak of a whine, his eyes switched down to her hand, then up to Bella's face, and back again. When he'd finally quieted some, she removed her hand and let him have his treat. He lunged for it.

Her cellphone buzzed and Bella fished it from her pocket. "Hi?"

"The house smelling like lavender and peppermint yet?"

"Hey, Lacy." Bella could never figure out why Lacy always gave her such a hard time about her love of essential oils. If she'd only try some on her back, she might be surprised at how they could soothe her aches. "That's a good idea, but I've been cleaning out the kitchen with lemon each morning. It's refreshing."

"I bet."

Bella gave her dog a quick pet and pulled herself up off the floor. "How are the wedding plans coming?"

"Swimmingly, darling."

"I'm so happy for you."

Lacy laughed. "Yeah, well, kiddo, I am too. I called to see if you'll be one of my bridesmaids."

Tears rushed to Bella's eyes. "I would love to be in your wedding. Thank you so much."

"I wouldn't have it any other way." Lacy's often-sarcastic tone mellowed some. "Four of us down, one to go."

Bella slid strands of hair behind her ear. She could have added her two-cent answer to that, but bit her tongue instead.

"So," Lacy continued, "what's it like having the bad boy as a servant?"

"I hope you're not referring to Rafael." Bella glanced at the doorway as if he would magically appear.

"Please. He's bad to the core, in the best way, of course." Lacy laughed loudly at this. "Some serious eye candy there."

Bella suddenly heard a male voice in the background of the call. Lacy's fiancé, Finn, was protesting something.

Lacy came back on the line. "Now see what you made me do?" She laughed again. "Finn's giving me a hard time about mentioning the town bad boy."

"You did that yourself," Bella said quietly.

Lacy sighed. "Listen, little sister, be careful. I'm serious now. Rafael can be a lot to handle."

"You and Maggie must be reading from a script. She says the same kinds of things to me, and honestly, I don't see it."

"Tell me you're not falling for the guy. Oh, Bella …"

"I'm not!"

Lacy exhaled. "Glad to hear it. Besides," she added, "you've always wanted a cowboy, haven't you? Don't settle. Trust me on that."

Bella could hear the smile in her sister's voice. No doubt Finn was nearby giving her an appreciative nod. Those two made Bella's heart swoon and pretty much contradicted the advice Kyle often gave her while grabbing the remote and changing the channel. "Life's not a Hallmark movie, Bella."

After ending the call with Lacy, Bella's mind continued down the road she had avoided since she'd gotten here. Truth was, if she had let things continue with Kyle in the direction that they were going, she, too, might have been engaged by now.

But he wasn't right for her, despite his dogged determination to convince her otherwise.

"You're just afraid of marriage."

"You've read too many romance books, Bella. This is real life, you and me."

And the one that sent her running for California as quick as she could pack a bag:

"You'll never find anyone who loves you like I do."

The first time he said those words, she believed him. She reasoned that he must have really loved her to say a thing like that. Right?

But then she would log on to the weekly video call with her siblings and see the transformation love was making in the lives of each of them. Though they would never believe her, Bella saw it all happening from afar, their countenances changing as love confounded—and then bewitched—them all.

She sighed, her heart quickening. Watching her siblings turned into piles of mush proved to her one thing: there was more in life for her than someone who said he was her only choice.

Still, Bella had not come here with a notion that the fifth time would be a charm, i.e., that her Prince Charming would somehow be waiting in Colibri Beach with a ring in his pocket. She'd only just realized her mistake with Kyle and wasn't about to go searching along wrong paths for the man of her dreams. Sadly, he'd been right about one thing: life wasn't a Hallmark movie. Look at Maggie and Luke. They were happy now, but how many years did that take?

Bella sighed and pushed herself away from the kitchen island. She refilled the diffuser with water and added a couple of drops of lavender this time and gently breathed in. She wandered over to the window near the ratty old couch and looked over at Wren's home. Maybe later she would walk over there and ask Wren for a few clippings from her garden. She could put those in a vase to compliment the calming scent wafting from her diffuser.

The thought of doing things differently from the way she had before, of making up her own mind without outside prodding, grounded her in a way she hadn't felt in a very long time. Breaking up with Kyle was the hardest—and smartest—thing she'd ever done. Yet, she had not shared it with anyone. Not even her sisters. She loved them all. Respected them. But it had become achingly clear to her that some decisions were better made on her own.

The sound of Rafael's truck rolling into the driveway woke her from her thoughts. She strained to listen, the sound of it louder than she remembered. Seabiscuit went on alert, his ears up, a low growl in his throat. Bella frowned and scooped the dog into the crook of her arm.

"It's only Rafael," she cooed. But when she peered out the screen door, she realized a work van was parked in the driveway next to Rafael's truck.

Rafael still wore that cowboy hat, causing an unreasonable thrill through her. He gestured to the man. "This is my brother, Serge."

Bella nodded. "Happy to meet you. Thanks for coming to help."

"He whined so much I had to."

Bella quirked a worried look at Rafael, who screwed up his mouth and sent his brother an expression full of daggers.

Serge laughed then. He pointed at his brother and shook his head. "So sensitive."

Bella patted Rafael's upper arm in solidarity but quickly pulled her hand away, both intrigued and taken aback by his strength. Slowly, he gazed at her, the unwavering look in his grey eyes unnervingly intimate. They stared at each other for another beat, until Serge cleared his throat, breaking the moment.

"This the one?" He nodded toward the couch.

"Yes." Rafael stalked over to the beat-up couch that had lingered far longer than most anything else usable in the house. "Help me get it to the truck."

Wordlessly, Bella stepped out of the way as the two men wrestled with the relic. Once they had a good grip on it, Bella, with Seabiscuit still in her arms, held the screen door open for them. They dropped the couch onto the driveway with a thud before she realized she hadn't seen its replacement, which was wrapped in a tarp.

The men worked in unison, wordlessly, though not without a grunt or two. Serge opened the tailgate and Rafael leaped onto the bed of the truck, positioning himself at the front end. He tossed his shirt and hat onto the top of the cab and lifted the wrapped furniture smoothly, easily. Even from the doorway she could see the smooth flexing of muscles beneath tan skin. *Oh ... my ... word.*

The men hauled the new couch inside, and Rafael's gaze

caught with hers as he passed her by, that same intensity from earlier. Bella blew out a slow breath as she re-entered the house behind them. Seabiscuit let out a whine and Bella realized she had been hanging onto the little guy tighter than she'd realized. She set him down and approached the guys as they unwrapped the couch.

Rafael balled up the plastic tarp. "What do you think?"

"Wow. It's so perfect, Rafael!" The inky blue fabric felt like velvet to the touch, with luxurious cushions and a long, tufted seat. She wanted to fold herself right into it, but hesitated, hoping the purchase was in her budget. If she were to spend everything on this, she'd have to make cuts elsewhere …

Serge stuck out his hand. "Good to meet you. I have a job across town, so I have to go."

"My brother also does steam cleaning of tile," Rafael said. "In fact, why don't we schedule you to come back here and take care of the shower in the master bath."

"Happy to," Serge said. "Now go put your shirt on. It's embarrassing."

After he'd gone, she smiled at Rafael who stood with hands on his narrow hips in her living room sans a shirt. "I'm glad you like it," he said.

"I love it." Another thought tugged at her heart. "I'll probably have to arm wrestle my sisters for it after the house is, uh, sold."

"Hopefully they will let you win."

"How much do I owe you?"

Rafael's eyes quizzed her, his mouth pulled up into a half-grin.

"For the couch, I mean."

"You may have it." He paused. "Let me rephrase that. Your family may have it now if you are allowed to keep it after the house is sold."

Bella laughed. "I'm sure they'll love the ultimatum. No, really. Just let me know and I'll get you payment for it."

"No charge."

"It's much too nice! Surely there is something I could give you for it?"

He grinned again, backing toward the front door. "Make a small donation to the shelter, if you'd like." Rafael jogged to his truck, whipped his shirt away from the roof, and slid it over his head and down his torso. Then he plopped his hat back onto his head.

When he returned, Bella flopped onto the couch. "I would be happy to make a donation to the shelter." She pulled a pillow into a hug at her middle. "Thank you again, Rafael. This is so beautiful ... I can't believe someone was getting rid of it in this condition."

Rafael's grin faded. "My mother no longer needs it."

"Wait. This is ... ?"

"Yes. My mother's."

Bella watched him, curiously. "She has lovely taste. I take it she is moving?"

A cloud crossed his features and he looked away.

"Rafael?"

When he turned, a resoluteness shone in his eyes, a soberness in his mouth. His Adam's apple bobbed, as if he considered a reply and then swallowed it back.

Finally, he said, "My mother is dead."

∼

SHE'D DONE what had come the most naturally to her. When Rafael revealed that his mother had passed on, she hugged him. Seemed like the right thing to do. But after several moments of her head leaning against his powerful chest, of listening to the solid beat of his heart, of wrapping him in her embrace, Bella began to second guess herself.

"Thank you," he said, pulling away from her. "Now, let's get to some of your projects."

She hesitated, but one brush of her eyes across his face convinced her that, though he appreciated her sympathy, he was ready to get back to work.

Truth was, her to-do list had barely been touched and she only had so many days left with Rafael as her helper. After that, she and Seabiscuit would be on their own.

For the next two hours, Rafael finished cleaning windows and screens upstairs, belting out an occasional chorus as he did. And Bella doubled down on the master bath. She also made a phone call to Clementine at the shelter, asking if she could meet for coffee next week. Bella had a couple of ideas to share with her before she left Colibri for good.

Somewhere in the middle of the day, Bella took a break to offer Rafael a bottle of water and slices of strawberries, which he'd accepted with an "all-is-well" smile, and then it was back to dusting corners of the house that hadn't seen a duster in ... well, she didn't dare guess. How had her siblings not noticed all that dust while she had?

So much for her being the laissez-faire baby of the family.

"Bella Boo?"

Bella spun around, and put her hands on her hips. "You did *not* call me that!"

Rafael flashed her a devilish smile. "I'm looking for microfiber towels. Have any up here?"

Bella sighed. "I'm not speaking to you."

He scooped up Seabiscuit and put the puffball in front of his face. "Bella Boo? Rafael wants to know if you have any microfiber towels."

"Argh!" Bella laughed. "Don't you dare turn my dog against me."

Rafael lowered Seabiscuit slightly and smiled into the face of the animal, who, much to Bella's chagrin, seemed to lap up all the attention. Rafael put the dog down and straightened, crossing his arms in front of his abs, the ones she was trying very hard not to notice through his thin cotton T-shirt.

Bella rolled her eyes. "Fine. No, I don't have any *microfiber cloths,* but I will add them to my list. Capiche?"

He winked. "I love it when you speak Italian to me."

"Rafael!"

He chuckled and stepped farther into the bedroom, his gaze traveling over the open, knotty pine ceiling. "Wow."

"It's nice, isn't it?" She drew up alongside him. "I mean, the house doesn't look like much from the outside, but I've always appreciated fine details like this. When my sisters were mean to me, I came up here and my parents always let me stay."

"You showed them."

She laughed. "Yeah, I did—my parents had a portable air conditioning unit. So you can bet I got mad at my sisters a lot."

"Devious."

She shrugged a shoulder. "Maybe. But I also didn't tell Mom and Dad about the wine coolers my sisters kept in their bedrooms."

"Wow. That's a lot of fuel you've given me on your sisters. And all I came in here to ask was if you had cotton cloths."

"Is that really all?"

Rafael shifted his stance, his dark eyes trained on her. "Should there be something else?"

Bella licked her lips, then immediately regretted it. The afternoon sun flooded the room, casting gold overtones across Rafael's warm skin and highlighting his edges and curves. The picture caught her breath, like an art piece might have in a museum or gallery. Quite suddenly, Bella felt as if she were floating on air, unable to draw an answer to his question.

Rafael's face sobered, watching her. "I think you need a break."

He'd saved her from her moment of insanity. Bella laughed lightly and dropped her duster into a bucket. "I think you're right."

They made their way back downstairs where the brightness of the afternoon further highlighted the blue variants in the fabric of the new sofa.

"Oh, Rafael, you really do have a good eye." She squealed softly, unable to help herself. "Your dear mother's couch looks so good in here."

"I'm glad you like it." He plucked the dog leash from the coat rack by the door. "Thought we could stretch out our muscles with a walk on the beach."

Seabiscuit appeared at Rafael's feet, as if he'd said the

magic word. He scooped up the animal, gave his noggin a rub, and set him back onto the floor to connect leash to collar.

A breeze ruffled the froth on waves as they rolled onto shore. Seabiscuit trotted on ahead, tugging on his leash, while whining and carrying on about a bunch of bitty sand plovers out for an afternoon stroll.

"Perfect day for a walk," he said.

"Pretty much every day is good for walking."

"Don't know about that. Can get mucky out here with thick fog sometimes. And I don't have to tell you about the trouble wind can cause."

"It does mess with my hair."

He laughed. "Yes. That's what I worry about every time I leave my house."

Bella let loose a string of giggles. He made her laugh and she hadn't realized, until now, how little she had done that in the past few years—even before her parents' deaths.

"You've lived here your entire life, right? Wind never drove you away."

"Not yet."

"I bet you would never leave."

He didn't answer her right away but kept his eyes steady on the shoreline. Suddenly they both spoke at the same time.

"Rafael, I wanted to ask you—"

"My reputation is—"

They each laughed. "You go first," Bella said.

Rafael gave her a sidelong glance, as if rethinking what he had been about to say. Slowly, he inhaled and breathed out again. "I was going to say that my reputation is no secret, darlin'."

"Oh. Well. I haven't seen any of that." She spoke softly.

"I'm glad to hear it." He went quiet again. "Colibri will always be my ... home."

Bella sighed, the sea breeze causing tendrils of hair to tickle her face. She slid wayward strands behind an ear and thought about her own journey to Colibri, away from here, and back again. At least for the time being. She'd left California years before because, for her, it was simply time. And though this brief visit to her former childhood home was mandated by her sweet parents' quirky will, she had recently reached the conclusion that it was, once again, just about time for her to go.

Only thing was, she had not decided where she would land after her month at the family home came to an end. No doubt the money they would all make would help her as she worked to set down roots, hopefully deeper ones this time.

"I understand," she said. "I only wish I could be as decisive as you."

He stopped and turned to her. "You came back to this town, and when you learned about the shelter's dilemma, you immediately found a way to help—"

"By buying a bachelor." She tried to laugh off his pep talk.

"Yes, ma'am. And instead of a week of dinner dates, you gave me something substantial to do."

She tilted her head, casting him a quick glance. "Wining and dining me would not have been considered substantial?"

A slow grin crossed Rafael's face, highlighting the deep

dimple in his cheek. His mouth opened, as if a reply hung in the air between them.

Once again, Bella questioned herself. Why did she say things without thinking? Especially things that could be misconstrued. She wicked a glance out to sea, her skin prickling.

He touched her shoulder briefly. "You deserve all of that and more, Bella."

She threw him a guarded look.

"I am serious about that. I know your family wasn't happy with our arrangement, but they are probably glad our time together did not include a week of dates after all." He paused, his expression sobering. "Though how would they feel to know how often you have fed me?"

"They would pity you. None of them think I can cook. I mean, cook anything that they would appreciate."

His smile returned. "Something else they would be wrong about."

A welcome spray of sea water dusted them as they walked beneath the sun's globe, the sand thick and spongy beneath their feet. With each wave, Bella replayed the call with her siblings, struggling to remember all that had been said.

"I'm really sorry I didn't tell my siblings you were at the door that night."

"It's not your fault."

"Still, it would have been nice to warn you. And, I'm sorry Lacy said you were flaky."

He didn't speak for a moment. "Is that all you heard?"

Bella's face heated. She was wading into waters she had never tested. Until now, her closest companions had been books and a pot of tea. For this reason, she hadn't been ready for Kyle, hadn't understood the dichotomy between how he, apparently, felt about her compared to how she felt about him. She liked him. He was funny. Smart. And though he wasn't a real cowboy—a fascination of hers that Lacy loved to tease her about—he liked the great outdoors. So that was a plus.

But Bella's skin never prickled when he was near. She didn't find herself lingering as she gazed at him, nor did she have an insatiable desire to ... cook for him.

When Bella glanced at Rafael again, his smile looked sad. Like someone about to say goodbye. He slowed and she did too, Seabiscuit tugging on the leash.

"The things they said about me were true." His gaze was hooded, heavy.

"Okay."

"Okay?"

She was tired of still feeling like a little girl. Like someone who knew nothing about how the world worked, how men and women found their forever bond. True, she had herself to blame for that, at least a little bit, but maybe it was time to stop assuming she knew what was happening around her. Maybe ... she should let herself ask questions.

Bella exhaled roughly and squared a look at Rafael. "Should I not trust you, Rafael? I mean ... with me?"

His expression faltered, as if he had been taken off guard. His eyes searched hers with concern and a softness that melted her like grass-fed butter.

Bella sighed and flashed him a small smile of her own. "That's what I thought." She took off down the beach again, a sense of something new and refreshing surging through her.

He caught up with her, the brush of his fingers against hers as they walked side by side, tension mounting between them. The good kind.

"I'm glad you trust me," he finally said. "I want you to. I mean, I want to know more about you." He exhaled and ran a hand roughly through his mop of hair. "But first, you had a question for me earlier and I never let you ask it."

"Oh, that was just an idea that I had. It's nothing."

"It's not nothing. Ask me anything, Bella."

She slowed to a stop and pivoted to look up at him. *My, he was ... stunning.* She exhaled slowly. "You said you know who owns that lot on the hill."

He seemed to freeze on the spot, but she trudged on. "Will you ask them if they'll let me bring up the goats to clear the land?"

Rafael's jaw hardened and she thought, perhaps, that she had insulted him. The idea had come to her and she had not been able to shake it ever since, as if divinely inspired. Maybe he thought she was using him somehow. She hoped not, but the more she watched him formulate a response, the farther the worry in her stomach sank.

Finally, he flashed her a brilliant, white smile. "You are the strangest girl I've ever met."

She leaned her head to one side. "So you'll help?"

This time, Rafael rolled his eyes. "Yeah, I'll help." Then he hooked one of his strong arms over her shoulders and kept it there as they continued their walk down the beach.

RAFAEL HAD NOT INTENDED on blurting out to Bella that his mother had died. But Bella's reaction did not surprise him either. She had leaped up from the couch when she heard and unabashedly wrapped her arms around him. Thinking about that moment now, Rafael flexed his hand around the steering wheel of his truck, the sensation of her touch still with him.

The rest of the day had been a tug o' war between torture and delight, a million will-he-won't-he moments. Truth was, he loved every minute of the simple grunt work she'd given him just knowing she was nearby. Not that he had voiced that truth in either word or thought. But the longer the day wore on, and especially after they had walked on the beach yesterday, their hands grazing occasionally, he knew it to be true.

He had been in this truck for how long? A half hour? Less? Whatever the number—it didn't matter—he had thought of her nearly the entire time. It was futile, this sudden daydream he was having.

For one thing, he had plans to clear out of Colibri Beach once and forever, to walk away from the memories and the mistakes. He would miss Serge, but his brother understood. In his own small way, he believed Serge wanted him to go and find the life that had never been theirs.

Rafael pulled the car onto the crater-filled dirt road and bumped along until he reached the grand sign: Sutter Creek Ranch. The surface of the road turned smooth as he drove alongside the paddock rails that seemed to run for miles. Without overthinking, he stopped his truck and hopped out. Sally, one of the mares he used to care for, stuck her head out over the rail, a longing in her eyes. It was as if she was asking, "Where ya been, Cowboy?"

He approached, almost sheepishly. Horses had a way of seeing right through a man, and Sally, though aged now, was not without that talent. Maybe even more so now.

Rafael ran his hand down the mare's nose and she sputtered a hello. He smiled with sudden emotion, raw and unanticipated. "Hey, girl. You know me, huh? Remember the good times we had?"

She winked—at least it seemed that way to him. He knew that she knew exactly who he was, and almost without thinking he clasped his hands about her neck and leaned forward for a nuzzle. "Missed you, gal," he whispered, his own voice husky to his hearing.

Reluctantly, Rafael climbed back into his truck and continued along the drive until a clearing presented the familiar, Mediterranean-inspired home. He hadn't been here since that one dark night as a teen. Some had said that night could be counted among his mistakes, but he'd never been able to clearly accept that. His wounds from that time, and even now, had yet to heal.

Exactly the reason he had made the decision to shake the dust from his boots and move on.

Rafael opened his truck door. He hopped onto the hard surface of the stamped driveway and strode to the front of his truck. He stood there for several seconds, hearing the rise and fall of his own breathing.

A meandering paved path led to a gated entry flanked by aggressively shaped topiaries. Beyond the gate lay a courtyard flush with pottery overflowing with draped flowers and water flowing from a sculpted child's watering can. His mother liked to describe the scene to him often, though she had not seen it in many years. How odd that nothing seemed to have changed.

A crackle behind him caused him to turn. His uncle, Ace Sutter, stood there, not quite as large and powerful as he had once looked to him, but imposing just the same.

"Planning to go in?" Ace asked.

"Don't have to now."

"I suppose not." The brim of his uncle's hat shaded eyes that were small and surrounded by lines that stretched down his cheeks. "Is it Marta?"

"My mother is ... gone."

Ace's expression flinched slightly. After seconds had passed, he nodded,

Rafael cleared his throat. "She went peacefully. In the end."

A flicker of something like pity crossed Ace's features before his jaw set. He flung open the gate. "Well, come on in now."

Rafael considered the invitation. How different life might have been if they had been a *normal* family. Then again, was there ever really such a thing? He turned his boots to the gate and walked the long path toward the house, hesitating at the front door.

"Go on, now. Willow will have lemonade and cookies, I'm sure."

Rafael turned a quizzical look on his uncle.

"Our cook. She took over for Patsy when she retired last year."

Rafael nodded once and stepped inside. He hadn't even thought of Patsy retiring, but it made sense. It's just ... she had been here for as long as he could remember, and for some reason, though so much time had passed, Rafael thought she might still be in the kitchen, apron on, baking bread or cooking up a stew.

Ace walked on ahead to the expansive kitchen with terra cotta pavers on the floor and Spanish tile work on the walls. "See here?" He pointed to a plate of cookies on the wide, flat island. "Willow didn't let us down."

A woman, much younger than Patsy, smiled gently. "Would you like some lemonade? Or tea?"

"Yes, ma'am. Lemonade, please." If this woman was anything like Ace's former cook, he knew better than to refuse.

Ace said, "Willow, I'd like you to meet my nephew, Rafael."

They exchanged hellos, though her eyes held surprise in them. No doubt she had never heard of Rafael, didn't know of his existence. Of course, Ace had a mess of sons, most scattered across the country as far as he knew. For a time, Rafael had felt like a brother to them all.

Perhaps Willow thought, at first, that he was one of them.

After she served him a glass of lemonade with ice and mint leaves in it, Willow left the kitchen. Ace eyed him but didn't ask any questions. Rafael had been practically a kid the last time he was here, when he'd spewed his anger all over the place. Guess it was up to him to start the conversation. To say what he'd come to ... well, ask.

Ace shifted, placing his feet wide apart, squaring his shoulders, as if preparing for battle.

Rafael could feel the tension rising in his neck. He took a

sip of his lemonade, to keep himself from blurting out words filled with old wounds.

"I've come to ask you about the property on the hill."

Ace lifted his chin, and in doing so, appeared to assess his nephew. "The one I purchased from your father."

For pennies, yeah ...

Rafael cleared his throat. "Yes. Do you still own it?"

"I do."

"Are you aware of its condition? That it's covered with weeds?"

That stiffness in Ace's jaw seemed to grow harder still and Rafael second-guessed how he had chosen to lead his questioning. Maybe he should have told him of Bella's plan. If his uncle could only see the delicate pout of her mouth, the way her big eyes implored, the light way she laughed about nearly everything.

Rafael nearly laughed aloud at his own thoughts. Bottom line, he doubted that Ace could have said no to Bella's request if she had come to deliver it herself.

"It's on my list to clear." His uncle paused. "Are you asking for the job?"

There was a dare in his uncle's voice. He could see it in his eyes, too. He believed Ace wanted to know if Rafael, after swearing he would never come back here, suddenly wanted a job.

Rafael's hands tensed, his fingers tightening. A debate went on inside his head over whether he should thank him for the lemonade and get back on the road without an answer.

Son, be quick to hear, cautious to speak, and slow to anger ... He heard his mother's mantra in his mind. She'd found the words in her Bible and said them aloud to him more than once.

Instead, Rafael lifted his chin. "Not exactly. But I know of a way to clear it that won't cost you a … penny." He tried not to wince on that last word.

Ace's eyes darkened, and mistrust layered in his gaze. "Son, there's no such thing as a free lunch."

"In this case, there is."

"Well, then. I'm listening."

Rafael drank down his lemonade, set the glass on the counter, and wiped his mouth with the back of his hand. He leveled a gaze on his uncle. "Goats. I have a friend. And she would like to bring goats to your land so they can graze and roam free for a while. Baby goats, actually."

"Goats."

"Yes." Rafael exhaled. "Sir."

Ace narrowed his eyes until the whites of them could not be seen. He popped them open suddenly and let out a garbled laugh.

"It's not a joke, Ace. The goats have been cooped up at the shelter for a long time. You have weeds on your land. I would think you'd find that a win-win situation."

Ace threw his head back now, his laughter rolling out brutally. "Cooped up." He wheezed as he said the words, laughing harder still. "That's good."

Rafael's anger dissipated until he struggled not to laugh himself. For the second time today, he wished that he had chosen better words to get his point across. Then again, the strain between him and his uncle was not the same now as when he first walked in. Still there, but the intensity had changed, lessened somehow.

Ace's laughter died a little. He smacked Rafael on the shoulder, like he used to do when he was a kid, and shook his head. "Yeah, sure, you can bring your goats on my land."

"Thank you." Relief caused the tension in Rafael's shoulders to ebb away, though not completely. His uncle had referred to the property as *my land.* It wasn't untrue, but it still bothered him to hear those words spoken aloud.

Ace eyed him now. "Are we good?"

He doubted whether his relationship with Ace could mend on this one point alone. Angry words still hovered between them, never taken back. Or addressed. Or fleshed out. For the moment, though, Rafael would be satisfied with receiving an answer to the question he came to ask, because now he could return to Bella with good news to tell.

"Yes. I'll see myself out."

Ace nodded and Rafael began heading to the massive front door, but stopped, pivoting. A question hung in Ace's eyes. Rafael set his jaw, determined.

"Before I go," he said, "there is one more thing you could help me with."

5

One day rolled into the next. Rafael had asked for yesterday off, and of course, Bella had not protested. After all, he'd offered her two days for the one he'd missed. How could a girl argue with that?

Yesterday, she had cleaned small spaces upstairs until her fingers ached from holding dust rags. So today she allowed herself a long morning walk on the beach. Even if she had wanted to skip it, Seabiscuit would have protested. When she lived in her Washington apartment, Bella had made a point to take her doggy for a walk regularly, but the soft lull of the beach's air and sounds had upended her usual schedule. After so many days in a row of work, Seabiscuit was having no more of staying indoors.

Up ahead, a congregation of sand plovers skittered up and down the beach to the rhythm of the waves. With no one around, Bella bent down and unhooked her dog's leash. He'd likely scare them a bunch but was otherwise harmless.

Just like Rafael.

Bella froze, the words wriggling through her mind with a gentleness she hadn't seen coming. Her bare feet sank deeper into wet sand as a montage played in her head of walking side by side with Rafael, laughing about goats, and debating the value of microfiber towels. Truth was, she was becoming accustomed to the synergy of working near him every day.

A buzz in her pocket pulled Bella out of her trance. She put her hand to her side but stopped when she saw how far ahead her dog had galloped, scattering those poor birds into four corners of the beach.

She cupped a hand around her mouth. "Seabiscuit! Come back!"

The unruly dog slowed but didn't turn around, a sure sign that he'd heard Bella's call, but was contemplating whether to heed it. She called out for him again, this time with the sternest tone of voice she could conjure up. Even to herself she sounded like a bird tweeting in the wind.

The phone in her pocket buzzed again just as Seabiscuit spun around and began running back toward her, his fur fluffed out on all sides. She watched the dog's approach, and satisfied, pulled out her phone and squinted in the sunlight at the screen.

A text from Kyle.

Bella deflated. His text said he wanted her to call him, to talk things out. Said he'd come to her, etcetera, etcetera. She never meant to hurt him. She had been proud of herself for breaking off things early, actually, before they'd become too entangled in each other's lives. It had been the right thing to do, although ... unfortunately, the discussion had not happened in person.

Seabiscuit appeared at Bella's feet, panting, mouth open, tongue out, and occasionally casting a longing glance back toward the wide beach. It was as if her dog was telegraphing a message: *You're missing out, momma!*

She needed to put an end to things with Kyle, once and for all. Bella exhaled and worked her thumbs over her phone's keyboard. She needed him to understand that she wasn't coming back.

She finished her text and clicked send.

Seabiscuit reached his paws up to her legs, his nails digging into her skin and leaving a trail of wet sand. She laughed, a certain relief flooding her, and bent down. "You are a goofy dog, aren't you?"

He licked her face and she laughed again. Then he hopped all fours back onto the sand and, with a quick look for assurance, began to trot down the beach. Bella brushed the sand from her legs began to follow him. She wanted to believe that her last text to Kyle would be her final one, but a niggling worry that it wouldn't be began to creep its way through her.

Truth was, she was drawn to Rafael in a way that she had never been to Kyle. Not that she would do anything about that, because, well, look at the problems with Kyle.

Their relationship had taken her by surprise. She hadn't admitted this to herself until recently, but Bella had, over time, become lonely. Her most adventurous outings were working at the library and then going home. She'd turned her apartment into a sanctuary, with comfortable pillows and layers of soft blankets. All of that had served to assuage the fact that, every time she made a new friend in her building, that friend would get married and move away. Or transfer jobs and move away. Or find a better living situation ... and move away.

Kyle swooped into her life a little more forcefully than she would have preferred. But his presence lessened her loneliness. He was attractive in his own way, a hulking figure with muscles that shaped his shirts and a tattoo of an eagle running the length of his arm. He liked to wear cowboy boots, jeans, and a hat—she had always liked the hat—and would come by almost nightly to watch football or whatever on her TV while she made dinner.

But after weeks of this, she realized how little they had in common. He liked monster trucks and target practice. She preferred riding her bike and eating vegetarian meals. Kyle listened to rock, while she listened to acoustic guitar music and other instrumentals. He liked the smell of barbecue, and she diffused essential oils in every room. Kyle wanted to know where she was at all times, while Bella sometimes turned off her phone and curled up with a novel and a cup of tea.

In the end, they were incompatible, and she knew it. After her parents' last wishes became known, Bella began making her plans. Once she her month at the beach house was scheduled, she quietly put in her notice at the library, stockpiled some savings, and traveled to Colibri Beach. In the end, she moved up her travel date to accommodate Maggie's wedding ... which led to a particularly abrupt end with Kyle.

Seabiscuit stopped to stick her nose deep into wet sand. Bellas smoothed back her curls, and breathed in the sea air, allowing it to center her thoughts. More than once, she had tried to tell Kyle about her plans in person, but every time she broached the subject, he would interrupt her.

"Kyle, I think you and I need to talk about our relationship," she would say.

He would silence her by cinching her close with one arm and smacking a kiss on her lips.

Or putting a finger to her lips and shaking his head. "None of that talk, now."

Or once, when she said she felt ready for them to take some time apart and said so, his face contorted into something that looked like extreme hurt tinged with a hint of anger.

She had backed down that time, unsure of how best to proceed. Then, in a stroke of the miraculous, he had been called to a work meeting some ten hours away. He had been gone a week, which gave her the time she needed to sell off her furniture and ship the rest of her things to a storage unit in California.

Even her family wasn't aware she had done that.

By the end of the week, Bella dropped off her key to the landlord, and with her bags and doggy in her car, she called Kyle, who was on his way back to town.

"Hi, beautiful."

"Kyle, we have to talk."

"This sounds serious. Why don't you hold on to what you have to say until I come over tonight."

"I'm leaving. I-I have a job in another town far from here." It wasn't exactly a lie.

"If this is your way of having a little fun with me, I'm not laughing, Bella."

"Kyle, we are just not right for each other. I think we both know that."

He paused, but she could hear him sucking in a breath. "I'll be the one to decide who's right for who."

"I'm so sorry. But I have to go."

She hung up before he could add anything more.

Once again, Seabiscuit appeared at Bella's feet, pulling her out of her thoughts. This time, his little face had taken on a surly expression. She forced a smile and bent down to give his head a healthy amount of petting. "You're trying to tell me to pay attention to the beach, aren't you, my love?"

Bella was about to continue their walk when her phone rang. A painfully sharp chill ran through her chest, and she peeled a cautious look at the screen of her phone. Rafael! Quickly, she answered.

"Bella? It's me."

"Hi, you."

"I have news. Where are you?"

That chill within her turned to a thrill and she smiled. "On the beach. Where else?"

He chuckled. "I can't say that I blame you. Want me to come to you or do you want to meet me at the house?"

Which would be faster? She sucked in a breath, micro-focused on wanting to see Rafael, to hear his news. She smiled fully now. "Where are you?"

"I'm currently on the back porch of the Holloway estate."

Bella laughed, picturing that. "Seabiscuit and I will be right there, okay?"

"You got it."

Minutes later, she arrived winded, her hair in loose knots from the sea's salt-laden breeze. Rafael was watching her approach, his muscular arms leaning on the wooden rails, a T-shirt thrown over one shoulder. She kept her eyes on him as she climbed the short rise of steps up to the deck.

He bent down to pick up Seabiscuit and his shirt dropped to the ground. Bella picked it up and threw it over her own shoulder, laughing as she did. His muscles shifted and flexed as he cradled her dog.

"You two look like you had a good walk," he said. "Did you?"

"We did." The text exchange with Kyle notwithstanding, but she cleared that memory out of head and refocused. "How about you? Did you have a good day off yesterday?"

He shrugged, but a tickle of a smile showed up on his face. "You could say that."

She watched him, searching for any sign that he may have missed … her. Her fingers fiddled with the soft cotton of his shirt until Rafael's grinned deepened. She stopped, suddenly realizing what she was doing, and whipped the shirt from her shoulder.

"Here," she said, holding it out to him. "This is yours."

He did the same with Seabiscuit, holding the wet, stinky dog out to her. "And I believe this wild animal belongs to you."

She giggled as they traded their *belongings*.

"Want to sit out here in the sun?" she asked. "Get some more vitamin D?"

Rafael dropped into a beat-up old chair and glanced at the tawny skin on his arms. "You saying I look pale?"

"I am not." She put Seabiscuit down and sat across from him, still smiling.

He pulled his T-shirt over his head, grinned, and leaned forward, resting his strong arms on his knees. "Good news."

"Yes?"

"I have contacted the owner of the property up on the hill and he has given us his blessing to take the goats up there."

Bella gasped. "Wait ... what? Rafael! Is that what you were doing yesterday ... Oh! I shouldn't be prying." She shook her head, not wanting Rafael to think he had to tell her his every move.

"You're not prying. Yes, I went to see the owner. He lives up the mountain, not too far from here, really, and I thought it would be easier to get a yes from him if I asked in person."

"Yay!" She leaned over and gave him a quick hug. "I can't wait to tell Clementine. She'll be so happy! Gosh, but we have a lot to do, don't we? We'll have to get a fence, I think, and figure out a way to get them up there."

"I've already picked up fencing material—did that on my way home yesterday. I'm going to build one that we can move around as sections of the land become cleared. And my truck is plenty big for those goats."

Bella shot to her feet. "Okay with you if I call Clementine right now?" She pulled her phone from her pocket and her heart sank, tempering her momentary high. A text had popped onto her screen. It was from Kyle saying not to doubt him—that he would find her.

Rafael stood. "Is something wrong?"

Bella looked up at him, her eyes unseeing. "I'm sorry. What?"

"You became so quiet." He touched her shoulder, his hand warm. "Is everything okay?"

"Yes, yes, of course." She slid her phone back into her pocket, as if doing so would help her forget that Kyle was not letting go so easily.

"Good, then let's tell Clementine when we've chosen a good date."

She looked into Rafael's face, his eyes fixed on hers, anticipation in them, as if they held a happy secret. She could use one of those right now.

"Why would we wait?"

"Because I have another surprise for you."

What more could she want? "You've already done so much, Rafael. I mean, I never meant to come here and ask for favors, but—"

"But I, your servant, am here to please."

He winked at her, and she nearly melted onto the deck. She knew he was still fulfilling an agreement, a promise to be her bachelor, aka handyman. She had to keep reminding herself of this truth.

Rafael continued. "I need you to do me a favor and grab your shoes and a beach towel." He lowered his gaze to Seabiscuit, who had found a spot of sunny bliss on the patio. "It doesn't look like he'll miss us."

Bella cast a glance at her dog, still wondering where Rafael was planning to take her. Oddly, she trusted him fully, and more than that, felt a rise of excitement at whatever his plans could be.

After she put Seabiscuit safely indoors and grabbed her shoes, Bella took her place next to Rafael in the cab of his truck.

"I don't suppose I should ask where we're going," she said.

"No, ma'am."

"I need you to promise me something, okay?"

"Anything."

She quirked a smile at him. "You don't know what I'm about to ask."

"True. But I'm sure it will be something I can handle."

"Oh, I don't know. I could surprise you and ask you to promise to take me swimming off the pier or something."

"Skinny dipping?"

"I never said anything about skinny dipping!"

"Sorry." He winked.

Heat rose in Bella's face, but she laughed anyway. "Quit teasing me."

He glanced over at her, grinning. "Okay."

"I would like you to not mention this outing to Maggie."

"Hm. Fine."

Bella tilted a look at him, his gaze focused on the road. "What's that tone for?"

"No reason," he said. "I completely understand, Bella. Your siblings aren't exactly my biggest fans."

"Oh my gosh, Rafael! That's not what I meant—I promise." She shook her head. "I just don't want Maggie to know I'm playing hooky from my responsibilities with the house. That's all."

He exhaled, then slowly slid a gaze her way.

She held his gaze with her own. "I promise."

He broke eye contact, snapping a look at the road again and then back to her. "So you're asking me to ... lie for you."

"Um."

Rafael's expression split into a grin. "Okay. I'll do it."

"You're ridiculous."

He laughed and continued driving along the freeway, causing curiosity to become front and center in her thoughts. After a while, he exited the road and drove under the freeway. She had never been in this area before and it intrigued her, the roadway dipping and rising as they moved closer to the beach. Foliage lined the uneven street, bending and bowing, increasing the mystique.

And then, the clearing ushered them toward the ocean again, a nearly-empty dirt lot waiting for them. Nothing but a couple of cars and a large truck and trailer parked nearby. Bella cast a quizzical look toward Rafael, a million thoughts crisscrossing through her, and yet, once again, she realized how much she trusted him. Whatever he was planning, she knew, would be ... amazing.

Rafael stopped the truck, turned off the engine, and hopped out. Seconds later, he opened her door and held out his hand. Silently, she took it, allowing him to support her as she jumped down onto the dirt.

He put his hands on his hips, considering her.

"What?"

"Wondering if you see them."

She tilted her chin up to him, laughing lightly. "See ... oh!" Next to the trailer stood a couple of horses all saddled up. One looked as if it had been dipped in luxurious chocolate and the other wore a coat of brown splashed with milky white. A guy about her age held the reins. "They're so cool, Rafael. Do people ride at this beach?"

"Yep." Rafael reached behind the passenger seat of his truck, pulling out two cowboy hats. He stuck one on his head and hesitated, then plopped the other one on her head.

For the second time, Bella heard herself gasp. "Wait." She

was laughing now, imploring him with a look. "Are ... we riding?"

"You want to, don't you?"

She stared at him, dumbfounded. A sudden, inexplicable knot formed at the base of her throat. Bella had mentioned, only in passing, that she had always wanted to ride a horse on the beach. He remembered that? And, somehow, made it happen too?

He quirked a grin at her and offered the crook of his arm, as if they were about to step out onto a dance floor. In some ways, maybe they were, only instead of a DJ spinning discs, they would be moving to the sound of the sea.

Bella took Rafael's arm, her heart lighter and fuller than she could remember for a very, very long time.

EVENING HAD FALLEN, but Rafael could not stop thinking about the expression on Bella's face earlier today when they rode horses on the beach. She smiled the entire time, her gentleness evident, even in the way she coaxed her horse along, patting his neck and cooing softly. She hadn't ridden in years she said, and never on the beach, but he could tell by her confidence that the lapsed time did not matter.

Rafael had made sure to plan their trip for when the tide was out, the morning cool. He had not planned to ask Ace to borrow the horses, but when he drove up to the house and saw the paddock and stables that he himself had helped to build when he was young, the urge to make the sudden request was too much to overlook.

So he'd asked, and though momentarily stunned silent

at the request, his uncle eventually said yes. Rafael didn't pretend to think that this meant their impasse was over, that they wouldn't, someday, revisit the reasons for their divide all these years. The expression on Bella's face, once she realized the nature of his surprise, made swallowing his pride where Ace was concerned worth it.

"Hey, Rafael." Stan, the bartender at Matty's Pizza, nodded to an empty seat at the bar and spoke over the blare of music. "Beer?"

Rafael hesitated. Then he flicked his fingers at the brim of his hat, pushing it off his forehead. "Make it a root beer this time."

Instead of the high he expected to be floating on after spending the day with Bella, Rafael found himself fighting off the urge to brood and alcohol would only help that along. The feeling came on with a vengeance after he dropped her off at the beach house with the realization that he had been daring to think that their friendship could turn into something ... more. They'd spent the day riding together, laughing, and talking. He learned that she worked as a library assistant part time and sold essential oils on the side, that she liked tending an organic vegetable garden, and that her favorite day—other than riding horses, that is—consisted of a book and an unending cup of tea.

She was everything he was not, and yet, he'd been drawn to her all day. Honestly, longer than that. Rafael knew better than to think they had a future together, though. For one, he had plans to leave Colibri Beach as soon as he could. A job waited for him, open until he could get himself to Colorado. If it weren't for the bachelor auction, he might have already packed up the house, turned his truck to the east, and headed out without looking back. At least that would have given him some downtime between leaving the coast behind and starting his new life.

Second, Bella's stay at the Holloway beach house was limited. Soon enough she would go back to her old life in Washington and the family house would be sold. He had not spoken to her about this much, but he sensed a yearning in her to unshackle herself from her family's heavy thumb over her life.

His thoughts turned surly as he thought about the finality of it all. But what had he expected? That somehow their ride on the beach today would cover over the obvious? No. He knew that today, this week, and any days they had left to spend together, were limited. He wasn't good enough for her. Her family had made that clear, and frankly, deep in his psyche, he believed it too.

Stan put the soda in front of him and Rafael wrapped a hand around the glass, staring into the dark fizzy liquid. A memory came into focus. How many beers had he had that night long ago when he'd confronted Ace? Enough not to care what he did or said, enough to drive a stake in the heart of his relationship with his uncle, one that had not moved in years. Even his mother's illness and death had not brought them together again.

His mother hadn't wanted anyone to know about her plight anyway, and he had done what he could to abide by her wishes—even though his reputation experienced an extra bit of tarnishing for the trouble. Then again, what was one or two more scratches on an already-scarred-up character?

He groaned, remembering the night that he had

confronted his uncle. After a couple of beers, Rafael found his way to the ranch. He woke up Ace and told him exactly what he thought of him, how his words and actions had pierced his family in the worst of ways. Ace hadn't taken kindly to it. On the contrary, he threw Rafael off the property and into the night's inky darkness. They had not spoken about the incident again.

Rafael shook his head. He took a long gulp, his throat burning from the sizzle. From the corner of his eye, he noticed a guy he didn't recognize commandeer a stool at the other end of the bar. *Probably a tourist here for the summer.* He blew out a rough sigh. The days of knowing his neighbors were dwindling fast. He tried to cheer himself up with that thought. No one would know him in his new town. They couldn't judge him by a reputation he'd created by his own bad choices.

Nor the one that attached itself to him beyond his control.

Rafael took another swig, mindful that the tourist was now bending the hostess's ear, loudly. Not that he could hear what the guy was saying, thanks to the abnormally high volume of music pouring from the speakers in the place. Just as well. Rafael had enough on his mind already.

He grunted, mentally diving deeper into his own to-do list. Lillian Madsen, his landlord, had sent over a couple of goons to assess his mother's home. She wanted to see how much of the security deposit she could keep, even though the woman had made it clear that, no matter what condition the house was in, she'd be fixing up the place. No doubt she planned to hike up the rent considerably for the next inhabitants.

Rafael had stood his ground and wouldn't let her guys in. He still had days left on his contract and he wasn't about to let that barracuda steal one minute from him. The hardest part to admit was, despite the plans he had made, Rafael wasn't sure he was ready to leave Colibri.

The music died away and Rafael lifted his glass to Stan in a toast.

The bartender laughed. "The noise was killin' me too."

"Excuse me?" The tourist in lumberjack clothing interrupted, focusing on Stan, who moved down the bar to talk to him. "Have you seen this woman?"

Stan looked at the guy's phone, frowning. After a few seconds, he shook his head no.

The guy twisted his mouth in disgust.

"Who is she?" Stan asked, wiping down the bar.

"My girlfriend. She came out here to see her family and I think she must've busted her phone. Can't get ahold of her."

Stan stood back, watching the guy. "That's rough."

"I'll say." The guy put his phone back into his pocket, tipped his head toward Stan, and slid off the stool. He surveyed the restaurant and headed for an empty table toward the kitchen.

Slowly, Stan continued to wipe down the bar, stopping when he landed in front of Rafael. He spoke, his voice low. "Did you hear that guy?"

Rafael shrugged. "Barely. Looking for his girlfriend?"

Stan's expression wore a mask. "If I'm not mistaken, the girl in the photo was one of the Holloway sisters. Cute, young, button nose." He paused. "Know her?"

Uncomfortable heat spread through Rafael. Bella had never said anything about having a boyfriend. Had she? His mind spun. Several times she had been distracted by something on her phone. A call? A text?

He snapped a look at Stan. "What did you tell him?"

Stan picked up his rag and began making circles on the counter with it. "Told him she didn't look familiar." He flicked a look toward the interior of the restaurant. "Something doesn't seem quite right about 'im, though."

Rafael nodded. He drank down his root beer and slammed the heavy glass onto the bar. "Appreciate it."

"You gonna mention it to her?"

Rafael licked his lips, thinking. "Might."

"Good idea." Stan turned around and dropped the overused towel in the sink. He pointed a couple of fingers at Rafael. "Another one? Maybe something a little stronger this time?"

Rafael held up his empty glass, thinking about it. He needed to keep his wits about him. "Nah. Another root beer'll do it."

Stan slid a full glass in front of him and whisked away his old mug. Then he made his way to waiting customers at the other end of the bar.

Rafael drank some of the soda down, the draw of it lackluster. He would have taken off but found himself stalling after the guy with the questions about Bella showed up. He could feel the stranger's presence in this place, and like Stan, something didn't feel right about him.

Rafael sighed and pushed the nearly full mug away from him. He signaled to Stan that he was leaving, but as he did, a pretty blonde blocked his path to the door. She had a look on her face that he'd seen before, like she'd been waiting for him to notice her standing there. The woman's long hair ran down both lengths of an overly tight blouse that framed her ... attributes.

"Hey, cowboy," she said. "Buy me a drink?"

Her smile was winsome, but it did nothing for him. In times past he wouldn't have even needed the smile to drop the first of many twenties on the bar and tell the barkeep to *keep 'em coming.*

"Sorry, Susie. Gotta go."

As he attempted to gently dodge around her, she pouted. That, too, would have been enough to get his attention in the past. But not tonight. Likely never again.

Rafael took a step forward, but Susie slid her arms around his waist and tipped a dazzling smile up to him, her hair swishing behind her. He couldn't concentrate. Wanted to get out of this bar. The sugar from the root beer had done nothing to clarify his plans for the future. In fact, he felt more confused than ever, dark thoughts compounded by the dufus who had shown up looking for Bella. Rafael had realized from the very start that he was not good enough for her, but that guy? Not even close.

"Hey, Rafael." Susie laughed up at him, pulling his mind from its faraway place. "Never knew you to be such a daydreamer. Maybe I could ride off into the sunset with you."

He forced himself to look at her, realizing that, beyond all control, his heart was somewhere else altogether. "Maybe some other time."

He removed her hands from his waist, stepped back, and tipped his hat before walking away. He had other things on his mind. The more Rafael thought about somebody else stepping in to claim Bella as his own, the more he dared wonder what he might do about that.

Realization thudded against his chest like a fallen log, blocking his path. Rafael could not dare to think about his own life without Bella in it.

HE HAD BEEN A PERFECT GENTLEMAN. Bella thought of nothing else since the moment Rafael dropped her off after his surprise. And what a surprise it was. She never would have imagined that he would plan a day of horseback riding on the beach. Never! Bella had mentioned her dream casually that day up on the hill, but more for herself than for anyone else's ears. And yet, he had cared enough to listen and make it happen.

A whisper of a sigh escaped her. How could she not sigh about that? She'd been floating on air for hours, and if she had to put it into words, Bella would say that, for the first time in her life, she felt like a princess. Or at least this was exactly the way she thought a princess would feel.

There was something else. Whenever she and Rafael were together, Bella sensed a tightening of the bond between them, an attraction to one another. And yet, unlike her siblings' fears, Rafael never did anything inappropriate. His touches were brief, supportive—such as helping her out of the truck—and occasionally laced with laughter, like the time he cinched an arm around her neck after agreeing to look into allowing goats to clear the land up on the hill. He'd rolled his eyes, too, and in him she was finding her way back to her old, carefree self, someone who would shrug and laugh and not worry about tomorrow.

After he brought her home and said goodbye, Bella had taken a shower to wash off the day's sun and salt. Now, as she padded around the kitchen with towel-dried hair, her stomach growled. She peered into the fridge but nothing exciting stared back at her. Rafael had brought them sandwiches and water, plus snacks, and yet, her stomach felt hollow, like she hadn't eaten all day. Bella also noticed a slight tugging in the muscles of her legs, a reminder that riding a horse for hours was a workout all its own. She shut the fridge door, and still heady from the day, decided to run into town for pizza and salad.

Twenty minutes later, Bella strolled into Matty's Pizza, the smell like home. Her mother's Italian food came to mind, and though Bella didn't care for meat these days, the aroma of tomatoes and garlic always stirred up a familiar, bittersweet sense in her.

The hostess greeted her. "Table for one?

"Actually, I'd like to order a veggie pizza and salad to go."

"Sure thing. Italian dressing?"

"Yes, please. Okay if I wait at the bar?"

"Absolutely. It'll be about fifteen minutes."

Bella smiled and thanked her, but as the hostess walked away, she made her way toward the bar and stopped. Rafael was at the far end, and he wasn't alone. A woman, tall and blonde, had her arms around his waist. Her hair flowed behind her as her chin tipped up, Rafael's eyes laser-focused on her.

She watched as one of his arms slid around the woman's back. As much as she wanted to, Bella could not tear her eyes away from the spectacle. It was as if he was in his natural habitat, comfortable in a woman's embrace. Bella's family had warned her, but she hadn't listened. Mainly because Bella believed in the live-and-let-live mantra. She had no claim on Rafael. He was simply a man she had bid on at an auction, someone who could help her fulfill her parents' wishes.

But ... he had become much more than that to her. She hardly could admit it to herself, but there it was. Until now, she thought she understood Rafael better than her family did.

"Excuse me?" The hostess had returned. "You're still here. Would you like to take care of payment now? Your food should be out soon but we've had a bit of a rush in the kitchen."

Bella blinked. "Yes, yes. Of course." She handed the hostess her credit card, thankful she could stay busy and out of Rafael's line of vision. He wouldn't expect to see her here, not after the day they'd had, and for some reason, she felt as if she was intruding on his *other* life.

"Here you go." The hostess handed her a pen. "Please sign."

Bella added a tip and signed her receipt.

"Can I bring you a glass of wine while you wait?"

"You know what? Yes. That would be perfect. Red would be great." Bella spied an open table by the window. "May I have it in the dining room?"

The hostess gestured to an open table. "Absolutely. I'll bring it over."

Bella settled into a table with a view of the street and gladly accepted the wine when it arrived. She took a sip and tried not to let her heart become tangled up in thoughts of Rafael and who the woman with him might be. She took another surreptitious look at them, her mood altering and the day's beauty beginning to tarnish in her mind.

"Bella?"

She jerked a look up, the voice eerily familiar. A man stood over her. Kyle? She blinked, disoriented. He looked out of place in this beach town, with his football jersey and heavy denim jeans.

He stared at her, as if seeing a ghost, his eyes unblinking, his mouth firm, as if angry. Or sad. She wasn't sure which emotion best described his expression, but the one she could count out was ... happy.

"What are you ... Kyle, what are you doing here?"

His eyes widened and he glanced at an empty seat at her table. "I've come all this way. The least you could do is offer me a seat."

She startled. "Yes, of course." Bella gestured to a chair. "Would you like to sit down?"

Kyle pulled out a chair, sighing audibly. She hadn't noticed before how dramatic he could be. Then again, his mother ran the local theater in their hometown, so he probably came by it naturally.

Bella held onto her glass like a security blanket. What was Kyle doing here? How had he found her? She kept a steady gaze on him, bolstering the courage to end this, this whatever-they-had once and for all.

"That was some trick you pulled." His voice was equally steady, his eyes spearing hers. But she had nothing to hide, nothing to be embarrassed about. She reminded herself of this, though honestly, all she wanted to do was pop a few drops of lavender oil in a diffuser, draw a bath, and feed her lurching stomach with dinner.

"Did you get my messages, Kyle?" She sipped her wine, hoping her stomach wouldn't rebel more, and waited for his answer.

"I got 'em, all right. But you don't get to decide when we get to break up." He slugged down a swig of beer and shook his head, his forehead so wrinkled it forced his eyes close together. "That's something two people have to talk about."

"Yes, but—"

"No buts." He reached across the table and put his hand on hers, effectively making it impossible for her to take another sip of wine. "Now, I came here to talk this out with you, face-to-face."

Bella let herself really see him. He'd been so genteel when they had first met. Polite. Used kind words. Patient.

But his behavior back then was no excuse for the rough display of it now, despite his disappointment with her. Hadn't she made herself clear? Her job resignation? The empty apartment? The phone message she'd left him? Bella shook her head. She shut her eyes for the longest two seconds ever and sighed. Enough. She was done being the baby of the family, the one who was never taken seriously.

Bella pulled her hand out of Kyle's grasp and stood up.

"Sit down, Bella."

She darted a look around for the hostess, hoping the woman would be bringing her food soon. When she didn't see her, Bella turned to Kyle and calmly said, "You need to go."

He stood in defiance, his skin flushed, his voice picking

up volume. "I came all the way here from Washington. You're going to talk to me."

Bella lifted her chin. She swallowed. She didn't want to hurt Kyle, but it was time she fended for herself. "Fine, I will tell you in person what I already said on the phone." She paused, mustered courage and looked right into his eyes. She hated seeing hurt looking back at her, but he had given her no choice. She exhaled. "You and I are not compatible, Kyle. You're a nice guy, but we just weren't working."

The hostess appeared at her side. "Excuse me. Your food?"

Kyle lunged for the box and sack and tossed them onto the table. The hostess's eyes grew large. Bella reached out to him as he took a step closer to her. "Kyle, this isn't the place."

He exhaled and nodded, calming himself down. "But ... okay. Right. Then let's get out of here so we can talk. Where're you staying?"

Gongs of protest went off inside her brain. She reached for her food again, but Kyle gripped her hand, preventing her from picking up her dinner, his expression controlled, a mix of frustration and sadness. "Don't you trust me anymore, Bella?"

She had to end this and do it now, preferably without making a scene, no matter how difficult she found it to be confrontational. Bella lifted her chin and leveled her eyes on Kyle. "I would like you to go."

He didn't move and his expression didn't change.

"The lady said she would like you to go." Rafael's voice cut through the tension. The restaurant chatter had quieted, no doubt, because of them.

Kyle jerked a glare at him. "This is a private conversation ... cowboy."

Heat crawled up Bella's neck, discomfort brewing from all the attention they were drawing. If she could have taken back her decision to step foot out of the beach house tonight, she would have. The day itself was ... magical. And yet, now she stood, between her past and her present—both of them making her question her ability to make sound decisions on her own behalf.

Rafael stepped in front of Bella, blocking her from Kyle's reach. His voice was stern, sober. "You need to go."

Kyle lowered his chin, like a bull. He squinted at Rafael, any perceived sadness quickly giving way to anger. "I don't like the tone you're taking with me."

Rafael reached behind himself and found Bella's hand, giving it a squeeze. "No need to argue about this, man. Bella and I were just leaving."

"Really."

Rafael gently let go of Bella's hand. He crossed his arms in front of himself and planted his feet in a wide stance.

The expression on Kyle's face morphed into a challenge. He shoved Rafael with both hands, not enough to topple him—if anyone could. Rafael returned the shove, but with more force. Kyle stumbled backward, a flash of shock on his face, followed by narrowed eyes. He threw a punch and Rafael's hand shot up in a block. He gripped Kyle's arm with one hand and blocked a second swing with the other.

Somewhere in the restaurant a shout rang out. Then another. Bella's voice mixed into the chaos, stunning her with its forcefulness. Another swing, and a block, both men on the floor now, with Rafael taking the upper hand.

She watched as Rafael yanked Kyle up by the neck of his jersey and shoved him outside. They were two men, strangers only minutes before, throwing punches and glares for those Colibri Beach dwellers lucky enough to have a first-row seat.

"I'll say it again. You need to go, man," Rafael said.

Kyle grunted and threw another punch. Rafael ducked, but it landed hard on his face—she winced at the sound of it. Rafael rose again and landed a punch of his own on Kyle's chin. He went down and in a blink, Rafael was on top of him, elbow pulled back, ready to land another one.

Bella grabbed Rafael's arm. "Stop it! Get off of him!"

Rafael stilled but didn't move.

"I mean it!" Bella yelled.

Rafael shook off Kyle like he was poison and bounded onto the sidewalk, towering over him now.

Waves of nausea stirred Bella's insides at the sight of blood trickling from Kyle's mouth. She didn't want him here —couldn't believe that he had followed after her this way. But see him hurt? Bella darted an accusatory look at Rafael, at the bravado he wore so proudly, and watched him recoil.

Kyle jumped up to his feet. He was breathing heavy, casting dark glances between Rafael and Bella. "This is the thanks I get for all the trouble it took for me to come find you." He spat blood onto the sidewalk and glared at her again.

Bella began to tremble deep inside, unsure if from anger or disappointment. Maybe some of both. The shudders running through her made it difficult to speak. She steadied her breathing. "You should not have come, Kyle."

Rafael moved closer to her, in protective mode. He slid his hand around her wrist.

Kyle narrowed his eyes again and attempted to dodge around Rafael to land missives on her. "And you should not have run off like that. Quitting your job? Moving out of your apartment while I was out of town? Had to guess where I could find you after I read about your sister and her billionaire fiancé building a place out here."

She sensed a shift in Rafael's breathing. She hadn't mentioned any of that to him, or to anyone else, really. Did he wonder about her plans?

Kyle shook his head and began to stalk away, shoulders bent forward, head down. Bella broke free of Rafael's grasp and ran after him. He stopped and pivoted.

"I'm sorry, Kyle."

"For what?"

"Hurting you."

Kyle shook his head slowly, a sarcastic smile on his face. "Too late for that." He jerked a look up into her eyes. "It's fine by me, though. Glad I found out now, anyway. I need a woman ... not a little girl. Bella, you need to grow up."

He spun away from her, got into his car, and drove away.

6

Rafael stood on the back porch of the Holloway house, holding a leaky pack of ice on his cheekbone, frustration and resentment pounding in his skull like a relentless headache. She had yelled at him—for fighting off *her* ex-boyfriend. A guy who had trouble scrawled across his miserable face.

Bella emerged from the house with fresh ice and an unchanged scowl, if he could really call it that. Her expression reminded him of a baby goat's. One stern baby goat's scowl.

"Here." She handed him a sandwich bag filled with ice. "Give me the other one."

Wordlessly, he handed her the drippy bag and took the new one from her. Finally, he muttered, "I was trying to save you, you know."

"I didn't need saving."

Rafael scoffed.

"Keep that on your eye."

"Stings."

"Good."

He couldn't decide what ached more, the bruise forming near his eye or the frozen shards of ice pressed against it. He was beginning to feel ... surly, his words falling forward without much thought. "Thanks for being honest, by the way."

She frowned.

"About the boyfriend. You left that detail out when you were telling me about your life."

Bella froze. Not the reaction he had expected.

What had he expected? That she'd punch a fist into her side and tell him off. Or cross her arms and tap her foot, her gaze haughty, her eyes flashing.

Instead, her chin trembled and those soft brown eyes of hers clouded with tears. She reminded him of a lost bird. Rafael's stomach sank like a rock. He had just taken a verbal swing at a ... lost bird!

"I'm sorry," he muttered.

"For what?"

"Accusing you."

A tear trickled down her cheek, a stricken look on her face. She sniffled and wiped away the tear with the towel in her hand. "You didn't."

Rafael leaned his head to the side, considering her. Now she really wasn't being honest with him. Why not just let him apologize? He lifted her chin with his fingers, imploring her to look at him. "Let me apologize."

She hiccupped.

He hid a smile.

Bella stepped backward and squeezed the water from the

rag in her hands. He recognized it as a way of making herself busy, of avoiding the conversation. He was a master at that himself.

"Are we okay, Bella?"

She snapped a look at him. "I forgive you, Rafael."

He nodded. *Good.* Still, something about the way she said it felt off, wrong, and his mind contorted with curious thoughts. "I want to ask you something."

She nodded.

"Why didn't you tell me you quit your job and gave up your apartment?"

Bella's face fell and her forehead bunched, like he'd just pried open a sealed can of he-didn't-know-what.

"Okay," he said, "I understand."

She didn't look at him. "What do you understand?"

"You didn't think it was any of my business."

Bella tilted a look up at him. "And why would I think that?"

He turned around so that his belly leaned against the handrail and his gaze stretched toward the ocean. She joined him at the rail, leaning into it. Rafael turned his chin, looking at her over his shoulder. "I consider you a friend, Bella. I haven't been trying to take advantage of ... of that. I know my place."

"Which is?"

He sighed, nearly exasperated. "Your friend, Bella. Or, at least I hope you think we're friends. I am not expecting anything more."

She was quiet, her expression pensive. After a moment passed, she said, "I saw you with your date." She peered up at him. "At the bar?"

A lightbulb moment. "Susie wasn't my date. Just a girl I know."

"Oh."

He growled a sigh. "Not everything is how it seems."

"You don't have to explain anything to me, Rafael. I was mentioning it because"—she shrugged—"you said you considered yourself my friend and nothing more. I'm letting you know that I didn't expect anything else either."

She had trained her pretty eyes on him, signs of tears and sadness marring her features. He watched her longer than he should have, the draw to kiss her, to show her how he really felt about her, driving him insane. But he held back. To her family's mind, he was a beast. In his mind, too.

How would it look if this beast were to suddenly sweep the beauty into his monstrous arms?

Abruptly, Bella stepped away from the railing, as if sensing the rising tension. The sudden, physical chasm between them created an ache in Rafael he hadn't seen coming.

"Have you eaten?" she asked.

"Not in hours."

"I'll cook for you."

He took her hand and held it in both of his. Couldn't help it. "I thought you were mad at me."

She shrugged. "A person has to eat."

"Yes, a person does." He frowned, letting her hand go. "Wait. You ordered food at Matty's. We left it there, didn't we?"

"Yes, *we* did."

"I heard that tone." He managed a chuckle and broached

her with a small smile. "Guess I'm the one who should be making you dinner, huh?"

"Well, I don't know. Can you cook?"

Something in her eyes taunted him, and for the first time that he could remember, Rafael had no idea how to read a woman. He hovered somewhere between whisking her into his arms and marching into that kitchen to make her a gourmet meal. He was leaning toward the former but knew better.

He returned her taunting gaze with one of his own. "I make a mean omelette. Unless of course you don't do eggs."

"I do."

"Or cheese."

"That, too."

"Or whatever else you have in that fridge in there."

She offered him a smile, the first one of the night. Then she put out her hand. Tentatively, he took it, but she pulled it away, shaking her head. "I was reaching for that melted bag of ice on your eye."

"Oh." Rafael handed her the plastic bag, droplets already forming on the bottom. Yeah, she had him wound up, all right. He would pull out his best cooking skills for her and keep his hands to himself.

Inside the house, Bella climbed onto a barstool and folded her arms on the counter. The kitchen her brother had created was spectacular. Rafael recognized the fine lines of the cabinetry, the high-end appliances, the carefully selected lighting. Reminded him of several properties he'd worked on, including his uncle's.

Quickly, he buried thoughts of his uncle and the ranch house he once spent so much time in. What's past was past.

For Bella's sake, and for the shelter's, he had made contact with Ace. That would have to be enough.

He pulled eggs, cheese, broccoli, and onion out of the fridge and shut it closed with his hip. Bella watched in silence as he hunted for tools—a bowl, pan, whisk—the works.

He tossed her a nod. "Not gonna help me, are you?"

"Nope."

"Penance, eh?"

She didn't respond. He conveniently kept his eyes focused on the kitchen counter and the omelette he was about to make, ignoring the occasional throb in his cheek. After cracking the eggs, adding salt and pepper, and whisking them together, he turned his gaze over his shoulder.

In the quiet, he said, "Are you going to tell me about the guy?"

"The one you nearly killed."

He laughed now. "Wow. That's some serious ego-stroking you're doing there."

"Something tells me you get plenty of that without my help, Rafael."

Ouch. Silence fell. If he had any question as to whether she believed the press about him, she just answered it.

"I'll take that as a no," he said. "As in, the subject of Kyle is closed."

"I don't know what you want me to say." Bella stretched out her hands, turning up her palms. "I tried to break up with him, but he wouldn't listen."

"So you left."

"It wasn't as abrupt as all that. I knew I would be coming here soon anyway."

"But you left Washington for good because of him, right?"

Bella sighed. "I never stay anywhere very long, Rafael. I tend to try on a city for a while and stay until it's no longer exciting."

"Like a new pair of shoes?"

Bella let out a tiny laugh. "Talk to my brother about shoes. He's the footwear hoarder in the family."

Rafael squinted a look at her. "Noted." He whisked the eggs over low heat. He would not have guessed Bella as someone who liked to move around. Just the opposite. There was something down home about her. He could imagine her moving into a place, layering it with her favorite things, and staying there forever.

He plated the food and served her first, then himself.

She cast a smile at him. "Good job."

"You haven't tasted it yet."

"Not talking about the food—I meant navigating the kitchen. I'll be reviewing this dinner on Yelp later."

He chuckled. "Make sure to mention me using my chef name: Town Flake."

She swallowed a bite of food. "Actually, it's Town Bad Boy."

Rafael considered this. "I'll take it."

Bella rolled her eyes and Rafael laughed.

"What was that about?" he asked.

"Nothing."

He leaned closer to her. "You're not scared of the town bad boy, I take it?"

She raised her gaze to meet his. "Should I be?"

Rafael looked into Bella's eyes, swirls of gold and milk chocolate staring back at him. He fought the urge to push away his dinner and pull her onto his lap. How much more sustenance did he really need?

Instead, he said, "Eat your food."

She continued to dig into the omelette, surprising him with her voracious appetite. The way she chowed down made him realize how truly tired today must have made her. First the horseback riding, and then the emotional upheaval at Matty's.

As if on cue, Bella put the back of her fist to her mouth and yawned. Again, he found himself in this disconcerting place of wanting to wrap her up in a blanket and carry her upstairs. He couldn't allow himself to think about what could happen after that, mainly because it wouldn't. The faith of his childhood had been kicking in lately, growing his conscience.

She yawned again, talking through it. "What're you staring at?"

He shook away his wayward thoughts. "Finished?"

She nodded and he took her plate and his to the sink.

"I've got kitchen duty." Bella showed up behind him.

He stilled, the feel of her behind him pulling at every one of his senses in a shocking way. This would be so easy, she and him. Every nerve stood at attention, the draw of her more powerful than he'd ever faced. Rafael didn't scare easily, but this ... this was new. Uncharted for him. The physical act of displaying affection was one thing, but exploring something deep, emotional, spiritual even, was not.

"You okay?" Bella scooted next to him, gently pushing him out of the way and commandeering the kitchen sink.

He stepped back, hands up. "Sorry. No. Was lost in thought."

"Oh." She seemed to consider that but then her expression changed. "So, Rafael, I was wondering if we could talk about the goats."

"The ... goats?"

She laughed now, flailing a towel at him. "Can't you read my mind?"

He was deeply confused. "Sorry?"

Bella rolled her eyes. "The goats that we're going to take to your friend's property? On the hill?"

"Right. When did you want to do that?" He'd forgotten all about it, especially with his move-out date looming over him.

"You forgot, didn't you?"

"No, no, of course ..." He looked into her smiling face and couldn't lie. "Yeah, I did."

For some reason, this made her laugh.

"Why's that funny?"

"My mom used to get so annoyed with my dad when he couldn't read her mind. I've also seen that faraway look in Jake's eyes when he has no idea what I'm talking about— even though it's fairly obvious."

"Is that right?" He moved closer to her, giving her a fake glare, unable to wipe away the smile he wore.

She lifted her chin, her eyes imploring his, unblinking. "Yes, it is."

He caught himself before he fell again into her eyes, afraid he would never recover from the drowning. Rafael took a half step back. "Well, thank you for reminding me about your baby goats."

"Baa."

He laughed again.

"So who owns the land? How do you know them?"

"I know the owner because, well—" he raked a hand through his hair, facing her question as best he could—"he's my uncle."

She seemed to startle at this, her eyes widening and then narrowing, as if confused. "Your uncle!"

"Yeah. We hadn't seen each other in a long time, so I drove up to talk to him before committing."

"Huh."

"What do you mean, huh?"

"Rafael, why hadn't you spoken to your uncle in so long?"

"You could say we had a ... falling out." He shrugged. "Not a big deal. It was a long time ago."

"That's so sad. What happened?"

His mind was beginning to swim with old hurts and half truths, which led to frustration. If he hadn't confronted his uncle that night, hadn't verbally sparred, what might have been? Would he be living the life he had once imagined? The life his mother had originally wanted for him? He swallowed back a sigh. Rafael couldn't think about that now. It was old news. The detour had been taken and he now had plans in place to move forward in an entirely new direction. No use reliving things of the past that could not be taken back.

Quietly, he said, "My uncle insulted me. I was a kid and didn't take it very well, so I told him off. He threw me off his land." He looked up. "And until the other day, I hadn't seen him since."

Bella stared at him long enough to see the thoughts turning in her mind, though he couldn't decipher her stance. Normally, he wouldn't care what anyone else thought. But now? He held his breath.

"Were you able to talk through your problems?"

"They didn't come up. He was fine with us taking the goats to the lot, so that's all that matters."

"You went up there to see him for me. Didn't you?"

She moved closer to him, and he couldn't take his eyes off hers. Didn't want to. She was right. If it weren't for her and her ... crazy ideas, Rafael would not have approached his uncle again. It had been a painful experience, still was, but he'd done it and Ace had said yes.

"So now you know more of my reputation is true."

"Oh?" She stood immovable in front of him. "What part?"

"That I'm a hothead." He licked his lips, still watching her. "A bad boy. A ... flake."

"I know nothing of the kind." Her voice brushed against his ears, a whisper he wanted more of.

They both hovered there, inches apart now, neither of them moving forward yet not backing away either. A thousand warning bells went off in Rafael's head, but he ignored every last one of them. He lowered his mouth to hers and kissed her, lightly, almost expecting her to pull away.

She didn't.

RAFAEL LEFT in a hurry last night, but not before he'd kissed her once, twice, and a third time. The look of wonder in his eyes did little to convince Bella further of his bad boy status. He had seemed almost as timid as she felt.

He thanked her for dinner, even though he'd been the one to cook it.

She thanked him for saving her life, even though it wasn't necessary.

He smiled at her, doffed his hat, and backed out the door.

Didn't seem like a Casanova to her. Unless he was a reformed one? She laughed aloud at the thought, causing Seabiscuit to let out a high-pitched bark.

She squatted down and rubbed his back. "Aren't you happy for me, Seabiscuit? Huh?"

He barked again.

"Fine, you big baby." She stood and headed for the coat rack to grab the leash. "I'll take you out."

Shallow waves rolled slowly onto shore, providing a soothing backdrop for their walk. A bit of haze appeared on the horizon, but it would likely burn off by noontime. After living in Washington for the past couple of years, and Oregon before that, Bella had become accustomed to mild weather. Unlike her sisters who liked to bake in the sun for hours each day, she preferred morning walks followed by afternoons inside with her books and pillows and unending imagination.

Last night was no figment of her imagination, though. Rafael's kiss on her lips had stayed with her, longer than she believed it could. Her heart sped up remembering that quiet moment with him in the kitchen last night. So unexpected. Until Kyle, she'd never had a boyfriend and never been kissed. Maybe shocking to some, but she'd never found anyone remotely interesting to give her heart to. And with Kyle, well, it all had been so, so … underwhelming. A tinge of guilt tweaked her insides. She should have halted things with him much earlier than she had.

Bella walked on, reliving last evening, both the fresh emotion of it and the new revelation too. It had surprised her to know that Rafael's uncle owned that empty, weed-strewn piece of property on the hill. Why hadn't he ever built on it? Or sold it? Certainly Lillian Madsen would have been after him to list it. And why hadn't Rafael mentioned his family connection to the land that day when they'd been up there together?

Still many unanswered questions for her there. The smell of brine and sea reached her senses, her muscles recharging, a renewed sense of energy reviving her. She never allowed herself to plan too far ahead, and yet, Bella was having a difficult time not thinking about the future right now. It dawned on her that she could not picture it without … well, without Rafael in it. Even though her siblings all found the loves of their lives in Colibri Beach, Bella hadn't aspired to that. She was just happy to know where she was landing next. All the other times she had moved she'd been in suspense about her destination.

Seabiscuit tugged at the leash, showing his impatience at the pace of their walk. She was not a runner or a sunbather or a mover-and-shaker like her siblings. She'd always thought that age alone played into her family's deep-seated need to "guide" her as they did. But maybe it was more than that. Did they see her differences as detriments? As inability to know good choices from bad?

She loved them all, truly she did, but she had learned to live by her own mind. Even though her mind did seem to change a lot.

After a half hour or so, Bella and Seabiscuit returned to the beach house. She unlatched her dog's leash and let him bound up the back stairs to his waiting water bowl. As she followed behind him, refreshed from their walk, she heard a boom inside the house. Bella leaned toward the back door, listening.

Rafael appeared and she yelped and jumped back, sending Seabiscuit into a barking frenzy.

He opened the back door from inside, laughter bubbling up from him. "Front door was open. Hope you didn't mind me coming in."

Seeing him there, looming in the doorway, threw her off-guard. Or maybe the memory of last night's kisses had done that. Bella smiled and looped a strand of hair behind her ear. "Not at all." Relief filled her that he'd shown up at all.

He landed a swift, brief kiss on her lips, staving off awkwardness.

She smiled and wordlessly padded down the hall, Seabiscuit in her arms, Rafael trailing behind her. It all felt so natural. The front screen door was propped open and Serge stood in the living room, a metal cleaning tool in his hands.

"Hey, Serge."

"Hey, yourself, ma'am."

She laughed and sent a questioning gaze to Rafael.

He grinned. "Don't tell me you forgot my brother was coming to steam clean the shower?"

She bit her lip and gave him a guilty little smile.

He chuckled. "Now who's the one forgetting?"

Serge cut in. "Is this a bad time?"

Bella waved him on. "Not at all. Your brother's just giving me a hard time."

Rafael raised his hands in surrender and laughed. "I'm not sayin' nothin'."

"Come on, Serge. I'll show you where the shower is while your brother stays behind here and congratulates himself."

Bella traipsed back down the hall, Rafael's laughter in her head, as Serge followed behind her. She showed him the old grout, watched as he assessed the possibility of brightening it up, then left him to do his work. When she returned to the front of the house, she found Rafael outside, removing the screen from the window on the north side of the house. Sweat glistened on his arms and her mind replayed Lacy's comments about the shirtless Rafael …

She cleared her throat.

He flashed her a grin. "I've been thinking about your goats. And I think early next week would work well."

"You sure you don't mind? I know I've been taking up a lot of your time lately."

"I don't mind." He cast a smile at her, his muscles shifting and flexing beneath his tan skin. Bad boy or not, family opinions or not, she couldn't look away.

"Okay." Bella watched him a minute longer—longer than she had to—and turned around to go back inside. She stopped at the small rise of steps leading back into the house. "I'll be inside if you need me."

"I'll come find you when I do."

Back inside, Bella called Clementine to tell her the good news about giving the goats a little exercise outside.

"Eek! You're the best! You and Rafael have really gone above and beyond, Bella," Clementine said. "You sure you don't need any help?"

"I think we can handle them. Besides, you have enough to handle with trying to get all your animals adopted. How is it going, Clementine?"

The woman sighed heavily. "It's hard, you know? But the people of Colibri are stepping up and for that I am grateful. Guess it took a calamity like Lillian to draw people together."

"Hmm. Still have to move though, right?"

"Unfortunately, yes. But thanks to the auction, we are paid up on rent and on the hunt for someplace new. Hopefully something'll turn up."

"Let's hope for that. See you next week, Clementine."

"Ta-ta, girl!"

Seabiscuit clawed Bella's leg. "So you're hungry? Use your words already." She laughed and grabbed his food from the cupboard and filled up his dog bowl.

Bella stretched and picked up her to-do list, carefully crossing off items that had already been done or were works in progress. She let out a happy sigh, surveying the kitchen. It was pretty spotless, thanks to all the work Jake had put into it. Both Maggie and Lacy had taken great care with it, as had she.

She crossed "kitchen" off her list and decided to open up the bedroom they'd all been avoiding, or so it seemed. The bedroom with the whale comforter had been the family favorite and they'd all either shared it or fought over it, depending on age or temperament. But the smaller first floor room that Bella had stayed in most of the time always seemed so dark to her, probably because it didn't have a window overlooking the beach. Some days she liked it that way, the room feeling much like a cocoon where she could hide away. Other times she simply felt left out.

Bella wandered down the hall, intending to tackle whatever she might find behind that door, but as she did, she heard the steam machine stop.

Serge stuck his head out the door and caught her eye. "Shower's done. Looks good."

"Really? A lot of grimy layers in there."

"Oh yeah. But you can see white in there now. Or at least beige."

Bella laughed at that. "I'm sure it's an improvement, no matter what. So glad you had the know-how to handle this for me."

"Thanks to my brother, I do."

"Really?"

"Yep. Rafael invested in my business. Helped me buy the truck. Proud of him. He paid Ma's rent for years too." Serge winced a little and glanced over his shoulder briefly. "Maybe I shouldn't be spreading that around."

"Your secret's safe with me." Bella smiled, her feelings for Rafael growing deeper. "Thanks again for coming out, Serge."

"Glad to do it." He turned and stopped. "Timing of all this has been great."

"Oh yes? Are you moving into your busy season?"

"Nah. I meant that you got here before Rafael left for Colorado."

She leaned her head to one side and tried to remember if Rafael had said anything about going on vacation soon. "Colorado?"

"Yeah, didn't he tell you? He's gotta job waiting for him out there." Serge shook his head. "Can't believe he's leaving me here, not that Colibri isn't great, but man—we've been in this area our whole lives!"

Bella kept a poker face, not wanting Serge to read anything into her surprise. "I'm glad too, then, Serge."

He nodded. "I'm just gonna go ahead and get all my tools out of here. You have a great day, okay?"

She nodded back, though how great it would be remained to be seen. Bella turned and retreated to the bedroom she was using and lowered herself to the bed. She ran her fingers over that big ol' whale, a million memories pouring forth from years before. How many times had she pounced on this bed just to hear Maggie tell her not to wrinkle it? Or Lacy call her a baby and chase her away? Grace was always sweet, but so smart she could be clueless at times.

Bella heard once that Lacy, the middle child, often felt invisible. To be honest, Bella sometimes wished she was. Like now. She and Rafael had just begun to form a relationship and he's leaving? She shook her head, not wanting to accept it. In the short time she had gotten to know him, Rafael had made her think that he really believed in her. She hadn't felt that in a very long time.

"There you are."

Bella jerked a look up to find Rafael in the doorway, watching her. "Hey."

"My brother left, so I thought I'd come find you to see what you thought of his work." He leaned against the door-frame, those smoky grey eyes of his intense. "You okay?"

"You're leaving."

"Oh no. I plan to stay all day and help. Did I give you the impression I wouldn't be staying?"

"I mean, the state. Serge told me you were leaving the state." She dropped her gaze to the comforter, suddenly feeling stupid. So what if he had kissed her last night and again this morning? She had done nothing to dissuade him, so it was as much on her as it was on him.

Rafael sighed and entered the room, dropping down onto the bed next to her. He spoke quietly. "I have a job waiting for me in Colorado."

She snapped a look up at him. "Why didn't you ever mention it?"

He didn't answer her, only continued to bore those eyes into hers. For half a second, she found herself daydreaming about life in … Colorado. She'd never been there but had always wanted to visit.

But he hadn't told her his plans, nor asked her to join him. She broke eye contact with Rafael and stood up. Bella had no interest in playing the part of the jilted girlfriend. They weren't even close to that. She rested a hand on her hip and looked out the window to the beach, gathering the peace she needed to deal with this news. Slowly, she returned her gaze to his. "You knew you were leaving this entire time. Even that day on the beach when you told me Colibri would always be your home."

"I will always think of her that way, but ah, Bella, there is much you don't know about me."

"Yes, well, I don't know what to believe about you, Rafael."

"What does that mean?"

She shrugged. "Why don't you tell me? You said the

other night that the woman with you at Matty's wasn't your date. We had just spent the day horseback riding and I thought …"

He reached up and attempted to grasp her hand, but she pulled it away. "What did you think?"

"I suppose you think this is, um, old fashioned of me, but I did *not* think that I would find you at a bar with another woman right after we'd spent the entire day together."

"And I didn't think I'd find you with some ex-boyfriend."

She narrowed her eyes.

Rafael kept his gaze trained on her. "You came here knowing things weren't over with him, but you were living as if they were."

"It *was* over with him!"

"Not according to him." He peered at her. "And I believe you said something to that effect after the … brawl."

"So you are saying that I bid on you for some other reason than to help the shelter and get myself some help around here? That I had ulterior motives where you were concerned?"

He cracked a smile that reminded her more of a wince. "I saw the women you were with: Kelly, Dani, and Casey. I know the things they've said about me, because they've said them to my face."

Her own face grew hot. Those women were fanning themselves at Rafael's very presence on that stage. Never dawned on her that Rafael would judge her by her association with them.

Ignorance was a problem with Bella, the truth of that reality sending a sinking feeling through her mind. She lived by her own thoughts and will and sometimes it knocked her on the back of the head, sending her a harsh wake-up call.

Still, she felt her will strengthening. Bella would not let him pin their actions on her. "I had just met them. They had an empty seat at their table, so I took it."

"I stand corrected."

Bella crossed her arms and let out a sigh. "I guess there's nothing more to say. None of this matters much anyway, does it? You're leaving, and frankly, I am too."

Rafael pulled himself up off the bed, drawing himself next to her. "When you first came to Colibri, did you plan on staying?"

She lifted a defiant chin. "Maybe."

"You've mentioned the different places you've lived. May I ask why you don't stay in any place very long?"

"I don't know."

"You sure?"

A tear showed up unannounced, but Bella whisked it away with her hand. She sighed. "To you, our life may have looked normal, but to me it was more complicated than that."

"No one's life is as it seems."

"Our family home burned down when I was really little and then we moved around a lot after that. Except for the beach house, we never stayed anywhere for very long. So maybe I just grew to love all that moving around."

"Or maybe you're afraid." He reached out to her, cupping her arms with his hands. "What are you looking for, Bella?"

She turned away but didn't resist his touch this time.

He nodded, licking his lips. "You said that you hadn't

expected to find me in that bar that night with someone else. What am I to you, Bella?"

Slowly, she returned her gaze to his. "I don't really know."

He nodded, his mouth and eyes sober. "Am I your hired hand? Or ... something else?"

When she dropped her gaze to the floor, she felt him shift and step back. "I get it," he finally said. "You think your siblings were right about me."

Bella's chin jerked up. "This has nothing to do with my siblings!" Why had he brought them into this conversation? And the women at the auction? She wrapped her arms about her body, hugging herself tightly. "You asked what I'm looking for? I'll tell you. For once in my life, I want people to take me seriously!"

"I take you seriously."

"If that's true, then why didn't you tell me you were leaving, Rafael?" A catch in her throat threatened to reveal her rising desperation. "You kissed me last night. Maybe that didn't mean anything to you—"

"Because I'm a flake? The town bad boy?"

"That's not what I meant."

"Then why say it? Of course, our kiss meant something." He raked a hand through his hair. "I've thought of little else all night."

"Even though you are leaving in mere days."

"Especially because I am leaving in mere days!"

She considered him, wishing she had more experience with figuring men out. He'd made no promises for the future. They had really only known each other a short time, so why would he talk about tomorrow? Yet it bothered her deeply that he hadn't said anything about his plans. He'd had plenty of opportunities to at least mention that he would be leaving Colibri soon. *And maybe even invite her to go along …*

Maybe, as she suspected, he never really had taken her all that seriously.

"Hey." Rafael tipped up her chin with the crook of his finger. "Don't shut me out."

"What more is there to say?"

His eyes dulled some and he dropped his hand to his side. "Can I ask you something?"

She nodded.

"Did you ever tell the rest of your family that I've not only been working for you, but that we've spent free time together?"

"Well, we haven't really spoken lately …"

"Uh-huh. I heard Maggie, you know. That time she was here and said she couldn't keep your secret for long."

"That was just Mags being … Maggie."

"Why are you so afraid of them?"

"That's a ridiculous accusation."

"Not an accusation. It's a question. Why are you so afraid of defending us to your siblings, Bella?"

With Rafael's gaze laser-focused on her, she almost missed the shudder of heavy footsteps coming from the hall-way. She tore her eyes away from Rafael to find Jake standing in the doorway, for how long, she didn't know. His eyes flared at them, as if they'd been found in a comprising position.

"Us? What do you mean 'us'?" her brother's voice bellowed in the quiet.

Bella spun away from Rafael, as if guilty. "What are you doing here, Jake?"

"More to the point, what's *he* doing here?"

Bella glanced at Rafael, who did not seem as ruffled by her brother's sudden appearance as she felt. "Rafael and I are just ... talking."

She thought she detected a slight eye roll from Rafael. He pivoted. "Your sister and I were discussing our relationship."

Jake shot her a look. "Is this true, Bella?"

"Sshh. Calm down, Jake. Rafael has been helping me around this place all week—"

Jake wagged his head. "Bella, no. You promised."

"He's been doing a great job and has made things much easier for me."

Rafael tilted his head, his eyes watching, his countenance changed. Finally, he said, "Glad I could be of service to you, Bella." He gave her a pointed look then, one that held a dare.

She bit her lip. "Don't look at me that way. I've done nothing wrong." She reached out to him, but he took a step back, his eyes still focused on her.

"Wrong, no. But"—he shrugged—"maybe Kyle was right —you do have some growing up to do."

She blinked rapidly. "Excuse me?"

Rafael's expression turned downcast, his voice tinged with regret. "Like I said earlier, I think you are too afraid of your siblings to defend us to them."

She rose on her toes, the start of a fire igniting in her. "And what 'us' are you talking about, Rafael? You kissed me last night, and today I find out that you've had plans all along to leave. Or have you changed your mind about that?"

"I have not."

The flames within her turned up a notch. "I see. Well, let me tell you something, Rafael. I may seem immature to you, but at least I'm not blaming all my problems on my family." She exhaled, her breathing suddenly labored. "I may not agree with them"—she pointed behind her at her brother—"but I'll never count them out of my life."

Rafael stiffened noticeably, a bitter tinge to his gaze. "You don't have any idea what you're saying."

"I'm saying that living for years near the same town as your uncle and being unable to make peace with him makes you look ... flaky."

Rafael licked his lips and swallowed, his Adam's apple jarringly pronounced. "You know nothing about my family, Bella."

She spun around, fully engulfed by angry flames now. "Ditto!"

Jake stepped into the room, in between Bella and Rafael, reminding her all too much about the altercation at Matty's Pizza the other night. She winced at the recollection.

"I think you better go," Jake said firmly.

Rafael's stern expression folded into a laugh. "Gladly."

As he stalked out of the room, Bella had to resist every fiery impulse in her to turn around and beg him to stay.

7

H̲ad she implied that *he* was the one who needed to grow up? Rafael gunned the engine of this truck. *Please.* He stewed and pounded the steering wheel, growing more impatient by the second.

This *thing* between them was over before it really ever got started. He coughed out a sarcastic laugh. What had he been thinking kissing her like that? Bella wasn't the town beach bunny. She wasn't here for fun and games. She'd swept into town with a honey-do list a mile long and a heart to heal the world. He had seen that firsthand in the way she'd stepped in to help the animal shelter without any regard to her calendar.

And he'd given her such a hard time about that today.

Rafael sighed and smacked the steering wheel again. Man, for the baby of the family, she could pack a wallop with her dewy gaze and quick retorts.

Rafael continued to drive, to think. In the past week he had cleared out most of his mother's house, had patched minor holes and made sure the place was cleaner than when they'd moved in years before. Old Lady Madsen could take their deposit, but he wasn't about to let her take his pride with it.

Frankly, Bella had already skewered some of that. He continued to drive up the winding road before him, with no destination in mind. He just couldn't go back to that empty house right now. Without his mother there, without all their stuff, it didn't feel like home anymore.

With no plan formulated, Rafael pulled the truck over to the side and parked. He grunted a long sigh and looked through a clearing to the big wide sea out in front of him. He hadn't even had a chance to take those goats up to the property yet. He huffed a laugh, thinking of those animals cleaning Ace's land. For free, no less.

Ace. Bella contended that not making peace with his uncle somehow made him look flaky. He sat back, still staring at the ocean, contemplating that charge. He wished that was the only thing that had tarnished his reputation over the years. Truth was, when his dad dropped out of their lives, even going so far as to sell land that might one day have been his, Rafael stopped caring what anyone thought of him. He did what he wanted, what brought him some sense of freedom and laughter in the midst of his mother's illness and all the fallout from mistakes made early in his life. He couldn't change a thing about the past.

But ... was it still possible to change the future?

Rafael rolled his hand into a fist, intending to pound on the steering wheel again. He stopped mid-air. Ace had once told him he was like his father—and it had enraged him. He'd said it because of the way Rafael got drunk and confronted him that late night long ago, but how was running away now unlike what his father had done to their family? The thought settled over him in waves.

He started the truck and once again began to drive, this time out of Colibri. He followed the curved, long, familiar driveway, this time less confident—and even less cocky— than the time before. He'd gone to speak to Ace about doing something good for the weed-strewn property. This time? Rafael was there to speak to his uncle about something altogether different.

"Get out."

Jake shrank back, his eyes popping open. "Bella? What's gotten into you?"

A tear slipped out of her eye, clouding her vision. She lowered her voice. Anger wasn't a strong suit for her, and she didn't like the taste of it in her mouth. She looked at her brother, pleadingly. "I would like to be alone, Jake. Please, go."

He must have recognized how serious she was because he left without uttering another word. No more questions asked, nor comments made. She released a sigh, thankful for the quiet. Seabiscuit slept in his fluffy bed next to the couch, seemingly oblivious to her turmoil. She thought about making something to eat, but nothing sounded good.

After a while, Bella wandered down the hall, intent on continuing to get the old house in shape to sell. She'd be doing this alone now, and though grateful for all Rafael accomplished, knew she would have to move quickly in order to get through her entire to-do list.

Bella stopped in front of the bedroom she was about to work on when Serge delivered her the news about Rafael leaving soon. She swung the door open and stilled, a slight scent of mildew reaching her nose. She flipped on a light. The room was as she had remembered it. Bunk beds on one side, neatly made, a floral reading chair, side table with a lamp, and a broken bookcase with stacks of magazines next to it. Grace had told them all about finding her favorite books locked up in the attic, as if they'd been kept up there just for her. She surmised that after she and her siblings had all scattered away from home, their mother might have taken over this room as her own.

She glanced around, not sure why that would be. Even with the light turned on it was still rather ... dark. Gloomy. Of course, that's what drew her when she was young and wanted to get away from her sisters.

Bella yanked on the blinds cord, the entire window covering pulling loose from the frame. It crashed onto the bookshelf, then careened onto the floor, sending up a plume of dust as its pieces crumbled and skittered across the floor.

Bella pouted. *Bummer.* Rafael would've known what to do, but she tucked that thought away. She would have to figure it out herself.

On her haunches, Bella reached under the bookcase first, finding a screw and a bracket—and more than a little grimy dust. She checked under her mother's chair next, not caring to add any more dirt to her hands. She frowned. Beneath the chair she spotted a shallow basket holding a stack of papers, old and curled. What were those? More magazines? With a grunt, she retrieved the basket quickly and pulled the stapled stack of papers onto her lap as she sat with her back against the wall.

She recognized her mother's doodles and handwriting instantly. The top page was a homemade cover of sorts with the words "Bella's Recipes" carefully written in a flourish across the middle.

Bella gasped, a ball of tears formed in her throat. She opened the cover, amazed to see many of her favorite meals written out on each page. Tofu burgers, brown rice and bean casserole, and avocado toast—before it became a mainstay in every kitchen in America. Pages and pages covered in her recipes and decorated with her momma's doodles, clippings of pictures from magazines, and even some hastily added notes, written in her father's hand, such as how to soften fresh rosemary from the garden in warm butter and her trick of adding sweet potatoes to roasted beets.

By the time she turned the last page, tears washed down Bella's face like a sudden storm. Her siblings liked to tease her for her eclectic food choices, but now that she thought about it, their mother had always been willing to experiment, to sprinkle in Bella's ideas to her already vast catalog of favorite foods. And her father had eaten them with gusto, as if she had placed a plate of his favorite spaghetti in front of him.

Bella climbed into her mother's old chair. She pressed the homemade cookbook to her chest, sniffling and reflecting. Despite this roller coaster of a day, a smile sprang to her face. Bella had never felt invisible. She'd come so late in her parents' lives that she always felt doted upon. If she were to be honest, they'd babied her. And she had loved every minute of it, lapping it up for as long as she could.

She twisted a look out the lone window in the room, the sun still unable to show itself through all those clouds up in that sky. Adulting, she decided, was hard. At any age. Her siblings still babied her, just like her parents had before them, and maybe Bella was being too hard on them for that. After all, each one of them had run off as soon as they could to begin building lives of their own, never realizing that ... she had too.

8

———

Three days had passed since Bella had fully taken the reins of the beach house project. She'd been doing everything on her list on her own now, even rebuffing a couple of texts from Rafael. She appreciated his offer to help, despite their falling out, but Bella had learned more in the past three days than she had in the last three years. She had used a miter box to cut new baseboards for her old room, hung blinds with new brackets, and caulked the surround of a bathtub. None of these chores were on her original list when she'd arrived in Colibri, but the more she cleaned, the more she found areas that still needed rehabbing. Somehow the work brought her a sense of peace.

Bella also scrubbed all the wood, touched up a few areas with paint that Maggie had left behind, and finished cleaning all the windows and screens. A pang of regret hit her when it came to the screens, as Rafael was working on them before he left for the last time.

She had even called Jake to apologize.

"Don't," he had said on their call. "I was being a jerk. Daisy told me so." His voice faded as he, obviously, leaned away from the phone. "Isn't that right, Daisy?"

"That's right!"

Bella giggled at Daisy's sisterly solidarity.

"Anyway," he said, "I sincerely apologize. Will you forgive me, Bella-boo?"

"If you stop calling me that, then yes."

He chortled. "All right. Fine."

"There is something you could help me with, though."

"As my punishment, you mean."

"If you want to call it that, you may."

"Fine. Hit me with it." He laughed. "What do you want?"

Now, days after that call, Bella thought about the agreement they'd made, happy that, despite the detour she'd taken with her plans, she had found a way to proceed. A knock on the door startled her.

"Wren?"

"Ta-da!" The old woman stood on the Holloway family porch, one hand on the railing and her other arm spread out wide. "I made it up your stairs without my cane!"

"That's amazing, Wren." Bella opened the screen door and the woman shuffled into the house.

"I'm so sorry I haven't been to see you yet, sweet girl." Wren patted Bella's face. "I've been quite busy helping Daisy plan her wedding to your brother. Looking at the internet so much makes me so tired!"

"Please—you don't owe me an apology. Can I get you some tea? Coffee?"

"No, dear, I just came over here to bring you these flowers"—she looked down at her hands and then pressed a palm to her rosy, lined cheek—"Oh, I must have left them on my walker. Will you go and get them, dear?"

"Yes, of course. Make yourself comfortable."

Bella dashed down the stairs and plucked the lavender branches from the seat of Wren's rolling walker. The deep purple blossoms sent fragrant memories to Bella's mind. "They're so beautiful," she said when she stepped inside the door. "Thank you, Wren. I remember how you used to bring these to my mother."

"Yes, I know. After we became friends, I planted more so that there would be plenty of cuttings whenever the Holloway family came back into town."

"That's so sweet." Bella filled a vase with water and plunked the tall stems inside. She stopped and reached inside the cookbook drawer. "Wren? I found this the other day. Have you ever seen it?"

Wren ran the pads of her fingers across the homemade cover. "My, yes. Your mother had so much fun putting this together. I believe I even loaned her some tape!"

Bella laughed lightly. "I found it under a chair in my old bedroom."

Wren nodded, a familiar smile on her face. "Your mother's chair—boy did she love that spot. When you were small and didn't want to sleep, she liked to tell me how she would sit there until you drifted off. Do you remember?"

Bella closed her eyes, thinking, the memory coming into view. A tear dropped down her cheek. She opened her eyes and smiled. "Yes, Wren. Yes, I do." She let out a small laugh. "I think she sometimes fell asleep too."

Wren rocked her head in agreement. "Yes, yes, she said that she often did."

Bella and Wren reminisced awhile longer, until the elderly woman began to show signs that she, too, was about to nod off. After she walked Wren across the divide between them, and saw her tucked safely back in her home, Bella readied herself for her family's weekly video call. She had much to report.

Bella piled a bunch of books on the dining room table and set her computer up at eye level. Then she searched for the link Grace had sent her and clicked on it.

Unsurprisingly, Grace appeared first, the glow on her pregnancy face simply beautiful. "Hi, Bella!"

"Hey, sis."

"We the first on?"

"I think so." A gust of wind scuttled across the porch. "Hold on. I'm going to prop open the front door before that old wind slams it shut on me."

When she returned, a third box appeared. Lacy was curled up on a couch in soft-looking loungewear, her dark hair pulled up loosely, a serene smile on her face. Such a change from her usually uptight self. "Hey, losers," she said.

Then again, maybe Lacy hadn't changed as much as Bella thought. She laughed to herself.

"What's so funny?" Maggie appeared, looking somewhat frazzled, but happy. She adjusted the camera, temporarily giving them all a bird's-eye view of her cleavage.

Grace spoke up. "Guess we're all here except Jake."

"Yeah, he's chin deep in wedding plans, I hear," said Lacy.

"As are you," Maggie said. "How come you two don't just have a joint wedding? Would be so much easier on all of us."

Lacy peered into the camera. "Because it's all about you, of course."

Maggie didn't blink at Lacy's swipe. "Of course it is."

"Well, I'm looking forward to both of your weddings," Bella said. She noticed Jake had finally shown up. "Oh good, Jake's here."

Her three sisters chimed in with their hellos to Jake.

Maggie began, "Why don't we get started. Bella? Do you want to give us your report?"

Lacy laughed. "Yeah, let's get this party started already."

Bella ran down the list of chores she had managed to cross off her list. When she began, a sense of elation over her accomplishments buoyed her, but as she moved through the list, mentioning those things that Rafael had tackled, her mood shifted severely. She had to take breaths more than once to keep her emotions from sudsing up.

Quickly, she put the list down and looked back up. "Any questions?"

Grace spoke first. "Wow, Bella, you've been busy. Thank you for all of that."

Maggie nodded. "Good job, Bella."

"Good thing I left the place in such good shape for you," Lacy said with a wink. "How about you, Jake? Have you been up to check out the place when you've been in town to see Daisy?"

Jake sent a *mea culpa* glance Bella's way. She sent him back a silent *I forgive you*.

He cleared his throat. "I have. She's done a nice job with it. I can hardly believe we're almost done with our five-month penance."

Grace cut in. "Not a penance—a gift!"

Jake laughed. "I was kidding. I've been reflecting a lot and realized how Dad and Mom always got their way. Even now."

Lacy held up a glass of something sparkling. "Here, here. I'm glad their way included me snagging a billionaire!"

Daisy peeked over Jake's shoulder. "Me too!"

Everyone erupted into laughter over those two and their fortunate finds in men who were both rich *and* lovable.

Maggie nodded, her smile contagious. "You got that right. I'm one happy woman and momma right now."

Bella's smile lingered, until she thought about the one in her life who had recently gotten away. She inhaled and changed the subject. "With that out of the way, I wanted to thank Jake for agreeing to help me with something in a few days from now."

"Ah, Jakey, what'dja do?" Lacy asked.

Jake put a weary hand to his face and rolled his eyes playfully. "She's making me pick up a bunch of goats from the animal shelter. Goats! Can you all believe it?"

Grace smiled. "Sounds like our Bella. What are you planning to do with all those goats, though? Not bring them to the house, I hope."

Bella chimed in. "It's a long story, but I noticed the animal shelter had all these goats with not a lot of room to roam. So I found a property where they can wander for a bit and eat the weeds. It's a win-win for the property owner."

"Yeah, and she's recruited me to be her goat wrangler."

"He thinks it's a dumb idea, but he's putting up with me anyway." She wished she could reach through the computer and give him a hug.

Jake's expression softened. "I don't think it's a crazy idea. I actually think it's quite thoughtful."

Maggie leaned forward. "Wow, Bella. I think so too. Kind of brilliant, if you ask me. Is this Lacy and Finn's property that you're talking about?"

Lacy coughed, nearly gagging on her cocktail. "What? Are you saying our property is full of weeds?"

Bella giggled. "Um, no. It's another piece of property, not as far up the hill as yours."

"The one with the steps going nowhere?" Lacy sat up now, as if curious.

"Yes! I was able to, uh, connect with the owner and he's happy to let the goats up there for a day."

Lacy nodded. "That's the coolest thing. Good job, Bella-boo. I took Finn up there once thinking he might want to put a boutique hotel on that lot."

"It's a great spot, but probably not big enough for a hotel." She shrugged. "I'm just happy to give the goats a little freedom. Hopefully the shelter will find new and better accommodations soon."

Maggie chimed in. "I have to admit—I saw her at the shelter one day with Rafael and she was like the goat whisperer or something."

Grace leaned in toward the screen. "You were with Rafael?"

"Oh!" Maggie put a fist to her forehead. "Sorry, Bella. I didn't mean to say anything. Now, Jake, before you get all cranky—"

Jake held up his hand like a stop sign. "I know all about it."

"Wait. You do?" Maggie frowned. "I read the paper every day and I didn't see anything in there about Rafael's death."

Lacy laughed, nearly spilling her drink. Grace put a delicate hand to her mouth, attempting to hide her smile.

Jake shook his head. "It's all good, ladies. Shall we move on?"

Bella licked her lips, watching them all banter. Every one of her siblings was happy—a far cry from their first call months ago. Since then they'd wrestled over issues and offered shoulders to sob on, they witnessed one wedding and cheered on another from afar. Some had made questionable decisions that were eventually accepted by all.

And now, for the first time maybe ever, they had lauded one of her projects. She really thought they'd all roll their eyes and laugh at her. Instead, they'd congratulated her. A swell of emotion caught in her throat.

Maggie yawned and Bella took that as a cue. "Before we all go, I wanted to tell you about something that I found." Bella swallowed back that rising tide of tears. She reached for the cookbook her mother had lovingly made and held it up for all to see.

"What's that?" Maggie asked.

Bella opened the book, displaying the spread of pages. "I found this in my old bedroom. It's, uh"—she stopped to control her emotions, gazing down for a second before facing them all again—"a book of my recipes that Mom made."

Bella held her breath, hoping they wouldn't all ruin this moment by falling into hysterics or mocking her food choices.

"That's so beautiful," Grace said, her voice breaking. "What a treasure you found."

"I'll say. I never even thought to do much with that room," Lacy said.

"Me either, for some reason," Maggie added. "I'm so, so glad you were the one to find that, Bella. Okay if I come by and take a picture of some of the recipes?"

Bella blinked. This was not the reaction she had expected from them. At all.

"Nice, Bella," Jake said. "As long as there's nothing with beets in there, I'll take a copy too."

Okay, this was more expected. "What's wrong with beets?" She laughed. "They're so good for you!"

He stuck out his tongue. "They taste like dirt."

Daisy appeared again and patted him on the cheek. "I agree that they're good for you. I'll have to find out from Bella how to make them."

Jake smirked, but she saw a light in his eyes. "See what you've done, Bella?"

"Yes, I do, Jake. And I'm feeling super proud of myself right now, thank-you-very-much."

The call erupted again in laughter, the sound like a balm to her fractured heart. The screen door rattled, as if caught by the wind. Bella thought back to the times their mother would sigh and set up puzzles and books for them to keep them busy on windy days. They would all whine and go outside anyway, only to come charging back in, crying about all the sand that blew into their eyes.

The wind outside howled louder, but knowing she'd have to avoid the beach today did nothing to take away from the boldness coming over her. She again glanced at the screen filled with her beloved family members talking and laughing together. Her siblings' love matches each came to be in the most imperfect way.

Grace caught hers by faking their engagement.

Jake caught his by making up for being a teenaged jerk.

Maggie found a second chance with the love of her life, despite the odds.

Lacy snagged a man who could turn her sarcasm into love.

Bella stilled. Maybe bidding on a bachelor at an auction, and finding him to be so much more than that, wasn't all that unbelievable ...

"Bella?" Grace's voice cut through her musings. "You look a little lost in thought there. Did you have more to say?"

She licked her lips, nodding. "I do, actually." Her heart accelerated, fresh boldness flooding her. "I was just thinking about all of you, and how you all, you know, found the loves of your life recently."

"Aw, Bella," Maggie interjected, "don't worry, hon. You'll find him one day."

Bella shifted a look at her eldest sister. "I already have," she whispered.

Maggie's forehead wrinkled and she moved closer to the screen. "Sorry. I didn't get that."

Grace eyed Bella. "I think she said that she already has."

"Whoa. Really, Bella?" Lacy swirled her cocktail in its glass. "Spill it, girl!"

Bella turned her attention to Jake. She rubbed her lips together. "Like all of you, I can pick my own guy."

Jake's expression froze.

"And I want you all to know that I, well, I want ... Rafael."

Jake sighed and hung his head.

The screen door flung open, and Bella bounded over to shut it before the wind tore it off its hinges. She skidded to a stop. Rafael stood in the doorway, his cowboy hat pulled low on his forehead, his eyebrows drawn down in determination, one hand wrapped around the neck of a guitar.

"May I come in?"

Suddenly mute, Bella nodded. Her heart began to do cartwheels in her chest. From behind, she could hear her sisters' voices mingling, chiming in with gasps, questions, and surprised laughter. She kept walking backward until she bumped into the coffee table. They were likely on-camera now, but she made no move to change that.

Rafael reached for her, his arms slipping around her waist.

She tilted up her chin, ignoring the callouts still coming from her siblings. "What are you doing here?"

"Doesn't really matter now, does it?"

The fluttering of her heart died down some. Was he coming to say goodbye? "I—"

He put a finger to her lips. "Shh. I'm not done yet."

"Okay."

"I came here to spill my guts, to tell you my story. But the bottom line is ... I'm not leaving Colibri Beach after all. At least, not without you ..."

Bella gasped. "What? Why?"

He smiled now, his gaze landing on her like a caress. "Because my hunch was right."

"Hunch?" Bella wagged her head, staring back into those liquid grey eyes of his. "I don't understand."

He ran his hands up her sides and took her face into his

hands, the tension between them causing her to swoon. His voice turned heavy. "You want me. I just heard you say so."

Laughter sprang from her lungs, followed by a spattering of tears.

His voice grew huskier still. "Am I right?"

Bella nodded quickly and wrapped her arms about Rafael's waist. "Yes. You're right," she said. "One-hundred percent right."

Then she rose on her tiptoes and kissed her cowboy with all her might. When she could finally tear herself away, her gaze landed on the guitar. She winked. "You gonna serenade me now?"

"My musical ability is limited to humming, darlin'" His voice turned huskier still. "This instrument here was my mother's." He paused. "And I'd like you to have it."

Tears sprang to her eyes. Oh, how she wish she'd met his mama. "That's the sweetest gesture, Rafael. I'll treasure it always."

He nodded and pulled her close. "Not as much as I treasure you."

9

———

y father was a gambler, a swindler too. He fathered two sons, my brother and me. Serge is my half-brother and never knew his own mother."

Bella watched Rafael as he poured out his family history to her, his eyes darkening further at times. They had come out to the back deck to watch the sunset, after the wind had died down, and seeing his pain touched her in a way she'd never experienced. "Are you saying that your mother raised someone else's child?"

"True. When my father's addiction to gambling became too much for him, he sold off the land that he had once promised to my mother, took the money, and left her with both of us—Serge and me. Serge's mother was someone my father met who had addictions of her own. Even though he wasn't my mother's—was a product of my father's affair— she took him in anyway. That's the kind of woman she was."

"She sounds like an amazing woman, your mother."

Rafael nodded. "Some said she believed too much. She told me once that my father said, 'Gonna build you a house at the end of those broken-down old steps.'"

Bella let out a deflated sigh. "But he never did."

"Nope. Sold it for pennies, my mother always said. I'd heard stories of my father gambling away our food money and the like. Eventually I started spending a lot of time with Ace, learning to build, to take care of the horses. When I was a teen, I learned that Ace had bought the property from my father."

"Wow."

Rafael hung his head, shaking it back and forth, the onshore breeze bringing much-needed calm to them both.

Bella continued, "Is it possible that your uncle was just trying to help?"

Rafael lifted his gaze to meet Bella's. "I had hoped that, someday, my uncle would gift the land back to my mother. Maybe that was the innocent kid in me, but anyway, when it stayed empty all these years, those weeds growing on it, my anger grew."

"And I made you go up there and face it all again."

"You had no way of knowing." Rafael reached over and squeezed Bella's hand. "As I have said before, my uncle and I had a falling out one day. I'd been telling him how angry I was at our father and Ace said something about my mother being an enabler."

Bella winced.

"Yeah. It felt to me as if he were blaming my mother for my father's sins!"

"I'm so sorry," she whispered. "Is that why you and your uncle hadn't spoken in so many years?"

Rafael gave her a grim smile. "It's worse than that. I would like to take this opportunity to remind you that you said you wanted me."

Bella laughed lightly. "Stop. It can't be that bad."

He eyed her, silently. Eventually, she saw relief—or perhaps resolve—cross his features. "One night, after way too many beers, I went joy riding up to the ranch with some friends. I remember it like it was yesterday." He bit his lip a moment, as if picturing it all. "I'm ashamed to tell you, Bella, that I woke up my uncle and told him what I really thought of him."

"You were defending your momma. No one, including me, would fault you for that."

"That's because you are an angel." He lunged forward and kissed her square on the mouth, the sound of it rocking in her head like a wave onto shore. He pulled away from her, a smile lingering. "My uncle then proceeded to tell me that I was just like my father."

Bella sucked in a breath.

"Never quite forgave him for that."

"Unforgiveness can tear away at a person, no matter what side you fall on."

"Yes. True. My mother became very ill and I should have told Ace. He was our only family. But ... I didn't. Strangely, when I drove up to see him for the first time in years, he knew. Must've been able to tell by the look on my face."

"Family members are good at that."

"Wasn't all bad. After my falling out with Ace, I had to find work, so I started my handyman business. I worked hard. Made a living."

"Serge told me you helped him buy his company van. And that you paid your mother's rent."

Rafael screwed up his mouth, his brows dipping. "When did Serge have time to tell you all of this?" He shook his head. "Doesn't matter anyway. I didn't do it for pats on the back."

"I know that. But it sounds like you had a very tough burden to bear."

"My mother was a proud woman. She did not want anyone to know of her plight, nor her lack of funds. There was a little money from the government, but otherwise ..."

"It was up to you to provide."

"I know this will come off like an excuse, and maybe it is, but the only way to escape all the pressure was to ... play."

"As in, throw off your shirt and run half-naked into the sea?"

Rafael laughed. "Who've you been talkin' to?"

"I know people."

He shook his head, a smile appearing. "For the record, I had to work very hard not to laugh in Jake's face every time he saw me with a shirt off when I was helping Daisy with her place. Made the guy so mad."

Bella giggled.

Rafael swung a look at her. "We probably shouldn't mention that around him."

"Probably not."

"Well, anyway, yes, I've been known to hang out on the beach, grab a couple of beers after a long day—"

"Kiss the girls and make them cry."

Rafael threw a *why me* look at the sky, then he swooped his arm around Bella's neck and tugged her close. "So we're clear, the only one I care to kiss from now on is you." He placed his mouth on hers and kissed her possessively, as if to demonstrate the point he had just made.

Bella laughed hard, pushing him away. "Okay, okay. I believe you."

He pulled slightly away, leaving a space between them. His expression turning pensive, sober even.

"What is it?"

"It still haunts me that your sister thought I was a flake when I didn't show up to help her."

"No worries."

"Yes, worries." He huffed a sigh, as if readying himself for battle. "That day was one of my worst ever. My mother could no longer care for herself. I had hired a nurse to help in our home, but Mom didn't want her there. It was not the best conversation we had ever had. We battled, in fact. In the end, I moved her to a home where she could receive all the attention she needed. She did not last too much longer after that."

"I'm so sorry."

He dipped a look at her. "And then there was no more reason for me to stay here. Until you, that is."

Bella sighed. "Oh Rafael, I ache for how hard your life has been. I can't believe that I asked you to take those silly goats up there. Seemed like such a good idea to let them roam free and clear the land, but now I see what it cost you to make it happen." She turned her gaze to his. "I see now that you didn't want to let me down."

"I did not."

They sat there, hands intertwined, the sea alive and beckoning. The sun had set, leaving behind an afterglow the colors of pink and fire. She leaned into him, embracing his warmth.

"There's more," he said. "And I wanted you to be the first to know."

Wordlessly, she looked into his eyes.

"I drove up to see Ace and we have made amends. He, too, had regrets, and we aired them all out, his and mine."

"I am so glad to hear that."

He nodded. "There's even more."

She sent him a questioning gaze.

"I have accepted a job just outside of Colibri." He dipped his head, his eyes fully on hers. "You are looking at the new foreman of Sutter Creek Ranch."

"The ... what?"

Rafael laughed. "You got yourself a legit cowboy, girl."

Bella lunged forward, hugging him tightly. "I'm so happy for you!"

"Thank you, ma'am." His deep voice cracked slightly. "Couldn't have done it without you, Bella."

"Rafael," she whispered. "I love you."

Rafael's breath caught. For a few seconds, he didn't speak. He brushed his hand down her hair, stopping at the nape of her neck. He leaned in, his lips hovering over hers. "I've fallen for you, too, Bella-boo."

10

———————

To our Beloved Children,

    If you are reading this letter, then the inevitable has occurred: Your mother remembered to put a stamp on the envelope!

Children, this is your mother. That was your father's attempt at a joke.

The truth is, your father and I have been in heaven now for at least five months—the minimum time it would take for you all to have fulfilled our wishes. We assume it's much longer than that, though, because as you know, the legal system is dreadfully slow. So perhaps we have been gone for much longer.

Whatever the case, we want you to know how happy we are, even at the time of this writing, that you have each come back to Colibri Beach. You know, suggesting you fix up the house was just our little way of giving you something to do while you were there. We are chuckling right now, thinking about you all putting your own touches on the house! (And as your mother, I hope and pray that you have not removed the whale bedspread. I so loved that. Alas, I am content with whatever you have decided. Carry on!)

Kids, this is your father. I have taken over writing this letter since your mother is starry-eyed after waxing poetic and all that. Let's get to the bottom line, shall we? The house is yours. It's always been yours. We wanted to make sure that you all had the opportunity to spend time in the place. I have every confidence that you have each done your best. You are all smart, intelligent, resourceful individuals, and your Dad loves you.

Children? This is your mother again. I agree with everything your father wrote. Everything! Oh, but I so hope you decide not to sell the beach house. Did you enjoy your time there? Did fresh memories come back to you and the love we shared there? Our life together was not without its ups and downs. We suffered much loss, oh, but in the end, there was the beach house that brought us together. Most importantly, there was all of us.

Kids, Dad here again. Do what you will. Sell it. Don't sell it. But stick together. Love each other. You'll get through everything that way. See you on the other side.

WITH LOVE ALWAYS,
  Your Mother and Father

P.S. This is your mother again. I know your father said we will see you on the other side, but take your time, darlings. Take your time!

T W O W E E K S Later

"I CAN'T BELIEVE we're doing this." Maggie sighed audibly, but her smile betrayed her. She, Luke, their daughters Eva and Siena, sat next to each other on one large beach blanket.

Nearby, Jake sat cross-legged, his designer water shoes sticking out above his lap. Daisy was on the mat next to his, barefoot.

Chase helped Grace lower to a mat, his expression one of doting concern. Grace, however, laughed freely, her nearly five-months-pregnant body landing on an array of nautical pillows that Bella had laid out for her.

"What a beautiful day we've been given," Bella said, glancing at the sky briefly. "I'm so glad you're all here!"

Lacy laughed at that. Though she refused to play nice with the rest by joining in, she had brought her camera to record the day. She stood on the inner edges of the fenced-in area, snapping photos wildly. To his credit, her soon-to-be husband, Finn, sat on a mat near Jake and Daisy, a good-natured smile on his chiseled face.

Rafael appeared from down the hill, a cowboy hat fitted snugly on his head, and a curled-up mat slung over his shoulder. Bella gasped at the sight of him, unable to control herself.

"There's Bella's sexy cowboy," Lacy shouted. She began shooting photos of Rafael as he entered the pen.

Bella gave her sister a mock frown. Lacy stilled and looked over the top of her camera. "What? You're the one who always wanted a cowboy. I'm just showing my appreciation." She stuck the camera in front of her face again and snapped away.

Bella laughed as she reached up and caressed Rafael's face, dark stubble covering it from long days on the ranch. He lowered his hat to block Lacy's lens and gave Bella a kiss that sent waves of adoration crashing right down to her toes.

"Excuse me?" Everyone turned to very pregnant Grace. "Beached whale over here might need a bathroom in the not-too-distant future. So sorry. Could we start?"

"Absolutely!" Bella turned to Rafael. "Could you let them in?"

"Will do." He flopped his mat onto the ground next to Bella's and charged back out of the gate and down the steps.

While he was gone, Bella found instrumental music on her phone, the sound of it reminding her of the melody Rafael loved to hum. She thought back to the guitar he'd gifted her, the one that had been his mother's, and her heart squeezed. Bella would be adding guitar lessons to her future pursuits.

She sighed and turned up the speaker, settled onto her mat, and glanced around at her family members, love and gobs of appreciation buoying her heart. She could hardly believe they were all here, together again, in one place. "I'll get us started as soon as Rafael and Clementine get up here. Just stretch a little while we wait."

A couple of minutes later, both Eva and Siena shot up to their feet, pointing and laughing and carrying on. "They're here! Oh my gosh! They're so cute!"

Bella turned to see Rafael open the gate and Clementine herd in a bunch of baby and pygmy goats. She laughed as one galloped right onto her lap, and another made itself comfortable on Rafael's mat.

For the next half hour, the Holloway siblings and their families stretched and planked and held poses as a dozen goats made themselves comfortable on and around them, laughter flowing through tree limbs nonstop. One goat chewed on Maggie's hair while another attempted to nibble on Jake's expensive shoes. Bella wandered over to Eva and Siena and showed them how to let the goats stand on their backs during tabletop poses. The girls giggled more than they exercised, their laughter so contagious that Bella found it difficult to focus on anything other than the joy on every-one's faces.

Hours later, after their impromptu goat yoga session had ended, they all retreated to the old beach house, with Wren joining them from next door. Bella threw open the windows to let the sea breeze flow in, as Grace, Daisy, and Wren collapsed onto the new couch in the living room. Eva and Siena took off to the bedroom lovingly dubbed the whale room. Maggie and Lacy retreated to the kitchen to pour drinks while the guys fired up two barbecues out on the back deck.

For her part, Bella stood at the kitchen counter, making salads, roasted brussels sprouts, organic corn, and black beans from the cookbook her parents had left her. She had already covered the pages in plastic, with the hope of keeping it intact forever.

Soon the kitchen island held more food than they could ever finish, though they were all doing their best. Some of them sat around the old dining table, while others huddled on the floor or couch, using the coffee table to dine on. Eva and Siena had eaten and run back to the bedroom to hang out with Seabiscuit.

"We have some news," Lacy said, breaking into the chatter. She glanced at Finn briefly. "Construction is beginning on the ghost house this week, thanks to our big brother over there." She nodded at Jake, who sat with Daisy and Wren in the dining room. The house had sat empty for years, and their name for it had become an inside joke. "Oh, and the crew is big enough that we'll be able to loan out some of them to finish the repairs on Colibri Beach Church."

"Such great news, and fast, too!" Maggie said.

"He's got a friend over in the planning office, you know," Daisy said.

Lacy cut in. "Yeah, Mel and her giant hugs say hello, by the way."

The room erupted in laughter. Mel from the town planning office was notorious for her all-engulfing hugs. She especially loved Jake ...

"Well, I could not have repaired my mom's house without his help—and Rafael's too, of course." Daisy sent a wink to Rafael, who laughed in response.

Jake rolled his eyes, but not out of animosity toward Rafael this time. Bella could tell by the appraising way her brother looked at her former handyman that they'd laid down their virtual weapons. She'd heard it in the way Rafael spoke about Jake now too.

"Does this mean the place will be done in time for the wedding? And wait ... will you be getting married at the little church?" Grace asked.

Bella cut in. "The one we all used to attend as a family when we were in town?"

Finn nodded. "That's our plan. I spoke to the pastor at Luke and Maggie's reception last month—"

"And the old softy was charmed," Lacy cut in.

Finn grinned. "Well, my hope is that we can spend the majority of our time here. I'm happy to continue the tradition of attending services where the Holloway family once did."

They all fell silent, no doubt reflecting on their childhoods. Bella sniffled, and reached out to Finn, patting him on the shoulder. "You did good, Finn."

Chase clapped, breaking through the solemnity of the moment. "That's good news!" He glanced at Grace then, as if for permission. She nodded back. He smiled and squeezed her hand. "Ever since your parents' beautiful letter, we've been thinking. And Grace and I have a proposal for all of you."

A miracle occurred: the room went quiet for a second time.

Chase continued. "We have made a decision to move our offices here."

Lacy leaned her head to one side. "Wait. To Colibri, you mean?"

"Yes, the whole operation," Chase said. "I fell in love with your sister here and can't think of a better place to raise our family."

Grace leaned into him. "We've already found a company to lease the building Chase owns, and we have plans to rent out our condo." She looked at her siblings, one by one, and sighed. "And to think ... a few months ago, I didn't even know how I was going to pay my rent."

"Me neither!" Maggie quipped.

Grace sent her big sister a loving smile. "We would love to keep this house in the family."

"So you want to move in here?" Lacy said.

"We would like to create a family trust to hold title to the house. We will lease the house from the trust, and if in a few years you all are feeling ready to sell, we will buy it out. Or we won't. Either way, we truly want to move back to Colibri —as a family." Grace glanced around. "If you're okay with that."

"Okay with it? I love it!" Maggie lunged for Grace, hugging her around the neck. "We're going to be neighbors!"

Bella joined in. "Our parents would be so happy to know a grandchild will grow up in this house."

Tears sprang from Grace's eyes. "Of course, the house belongs to all of us. I want Eva and Siena to feel at home here."

Luke smiled. "They'd love that."

Lacy glanced at Bella. "What about you, kiddo? I'm guessing you won't be doing your normal thing and flying off to some unknown place anytime soon."

Rafael snugged her in for a side hug. "Not if I have anything to say about it."

Bella nodded. She glanced around at the puzzle of her family, all the pieces nearly in place. "That's right, everyone. Jake knows this already, but we haven't told you all yet. Rafael will be building a barn with an apartment on the lot —Jake's helping with the plans for that too. Rafael will lease the barn back to the shelter for five years while they search out a more permanent home."

"Shoot, Jakey," Lacy said, "how many hugs did you have to give Mel in the planning office for that zoning change?"

"Ha ha ha." Jake shook his head. "Why do I put up with you?"

"Anyway," Bella said, cutting back into the conversation. "As you all know, Rafael is living at Sutter Creek Ranch now in one of the guest houses. His place is so nice, you guys! He's going to let me stay in the barn apartment, once it's built. So," she looked at Grace, "I know we talked about this already. Still okay if I bunk with you guys for a short while?"

"Of course!" Grace clasped her hands. "The more the merrier."

Rafael removed his hat and cleared his throat. "There have been some changes."

Bella swiveled around to face him, searching his eyes. "Really? But I thought it was all decided."

He shook his head, that, indeed, some changes had been made.

"Oh." Bella swallowed, not sure what to say.

A grin broke across Rafael's face, as if he could not contain it. He folded his strong hands around Bella's and dropped to one knee. "I want you to live with me. On the ranch."

The whole room had gone silent, except for the unmistakable presence of Eva and Siena emerging from down the hall, their footsteps falling on wooden floors, reminiscent of times past.

Rafael continued to gaze up at Bella, massaging her fingers with his. "I have a question for you, Bella."

Bella fell silent, the shudder of her heartbeat filling her head with wonder.

"You've tamed me, Bella. Taught me how to love and to forgive, and to grab onto the future with more hope than this thick-headed cowboy thought he'd ever have." He paused, an unmovable expression of love imploring her. "I love you, Bella. With everything I've got. Will you marry me?"

No longer able to contain the stirring of emotion within her, Bella squealed, the sound of it suddenly contagious. Before she could deliver her answer, all three of her sisters were around her, hugging her neck and offering their congratulations. In the midst of the onslaught, Rafael had fallen away to let Siena and Eva join in the celebration, hugging her around the waist with their skinny little arms.

Jake approached them all, and through Bella's tears, she could see the soberness of his expression. He calmly reached into the group hug and put a hand on Bella's shoulder. Then he gazed at each one of his sisters in turn. "She hasn't even given the poor guy an answer yet."

A shout of laughter went up, each one of them giving her one more squeeze before backing away. They parted to reveal Rafael standing there, his hat back on his head now, his smoke-grey eyes still holding a question.

Giddy, she bit her bottom lip, unable to stop smiling. Bella lunged forward, wrapped her arms around him, and lifted her chin.

His arm curved behind her waist, and his voice turned huskier. "So? Will you?"

"I thought you'd never ask." A smile curled her lips. "My answer is ... yes!"

Rafael sent out a howl as he scooped up Bella into his

arms, pressing his lips to hers, that familiar hum of his resonating through her. It was music to her ears. Bella had never felt so grounded in her life. She no longer felt the desire to move away again, or to seek all that was missing. Why would she?

Everything she ever wanted was here: family, home—and a future with her cowboy.

ACKNOWLEDGMENTS

Thank you for reading this final installment of the Beach House Romance series. I hope you've had a chance to read all five books, and that you've fallen in love with the Holloway siblings as I have!

If I'm new to you, welcome! I began my novel-writing career years ago with a chick-lit novel called *Chocolate Beach*. Since then, I've written romantic women's fiction, cozy mysteries, and most recently with this series, contemporary romance!

Join my reader community and I'll send you a free e-novella just for signing up. You can find that here: Julie-Carobini.com - Free Book.

Thank you again, and as always ... cheers from the coast!

Julie

ALSO BY JULIE CAROBINI

Julie's books are available wherever books are sold, including her online shop: JulieCarobini.com

This is her complete list at time of publication.

Beach House Romances

Beach Sunrise (book 1)

Beach Memories (book 2)

Beach Secrets (book 3)

Beach Sunset (book 4)

Beach Music (book 5)

Standalone

Reunion in Saltwater Beach

Hollywood by the Sea Novels

Chasing Valentino (book 1)

Finding Stardust (book 2)

Sea Glass Inn Novels

Walking on Sea Glass (book 1)

Runaway Tide (book 2)

Windswept (book 3)

Beneath a Billion Stars (book 4)

A Sea Glass Christmas (book 5)

<u>Otter Bay Novels</u>

Sweet Waters (book 1)

A Shore Thing (book 2)

Fade to Blue (book 3)

The Otter Bay Novel Collection (books 1-3)

<u>The Chocolate Series</u>

Chocolate Beach (book 1)

Truffles by the Sea (book 2)

Mocha Sunrise (book 3)

<u>Cottage Grove Cozy Mysteries</u>

The Christmas Thief (book 1)

The Christmas Killer (book 2)

The Christmas Heist (book 3)

Cottage Grove Mysteries (books 1-3)

ABOUT THE AUTHOR

JULIE CAROBINI is the author of 22+ inspirational beach romances. Her books feature captivating heroines, endearing heroes, and a cast of quirky friends, all bound together by the secrets they keep. Her bestselling titles include *Walking on Sea Glass*, *Runaway Tide*, and *Reunion in Saltwater Beach*. Julie has received awards for writing and editing from The National League of American Pen Women and ACFW, and she is a double finalist for the ACFW Carol Award. She is the mother of three grown kids and lives on the California coast with her husband, Dan, and their rescue pup, Dancer.

Please visit her at
www.juliecarobini.com